# Gardener Winter

Also by nova

*American Apocalypse: Beginnings*
*American Apocalypse: Refuge*
*Gardener Summer*
*American Apocalypse: Migration*
*American Apocalypse: Rescue*
*The Chosen*
*Diary of a Serial Killer*

# Gardener Winter

by

# NOVA

Blackheart Publications

First published in 2012 by Blackheart
Publications.
Previously published in unedited form online
at http://theamericanapocalypse.blogspot.com.

ISBN-10: 1469967286
ISBN-13: 978-1469967288

First Edition: January 2012
Printed in the United States of America

For Marilyn and Elizabeth

# Acknowledgements

Thanks as always to Bill McBride of Calculated Risk.
Tanta Vive!

To my readers, especially those who read it online, and offered suggestions and comments. Thank you very much!

Kristy, the editor!

# Gardener Winter

# Chapter One

I came down the side of the hill the hard way. I walked. It had been a while since I had walked any distance, and it took me all of six steps to remember why. My boot leather was in sad shape, but the soles were even worse. I probably would have taken them off and tossed them out of anger and frustration but, common sense, something that is not a natural thing with me, prevailed. The little voice in my head whispered, *"Hey, dumb shit...that's your only pair."* It's tough to argue with logic like that. Though, when the left heel came off the second time, it was a close call. The third time I stopped, picked up the heel, and sat down. I pulled my boot off, stared at where it was supposed to have stayed attached, and laughed my ass off. When I was done I sat there, stared off into the distance, looked at the heel and laughed some more.

Life is a bitch. You take it too seriously and you'll end up fighting for a cause or worse – dying for one. Lord knows I had learned that the hard way. I was a veteran in a world where everyone nowadays was a veteran of organized violence. The only difference was I was an old veteran and there were not many of us around. Why? You spent long enough doing this for a living, and eventually bad luck or someone faster crossed your path.

I had worn different uniforms in different places and fought in everything from skirmishes to battles. I liked wearing a uniform. It eliminated another problem in my life at the time, which was having decent clothes to wear. It also cut down on any color coordination and style choices I needed to make.

I had to get rid of of most of my last uniform. When your side loses it helps not to identify yourself as a recent participant, let alone former member of a unit that was regarded as an elite unit by the losers and as a band of terrorists by the winners. I held on to my boots long after I should have dumped them and bought another pair. Why? Because they were from back then, the time when I believed, when defeat was never an option and victory was still a possibility. In the moments when I was honest with myself I knew, even if we had won that battle, I had still lost. I still kept doing it. Why? Because I didn't know anything else, and because I was very good at it. Which was another reason I was sitting out here in the middle of nowhere thirsty, footsore, and hungry.

I had come a long way in an even longer time since the early days when I first started down the road that defined my life. Now here I was, sitting on a rock in the middle of nowhere and running behind schedule. It shouldn't bother me, but it did. I had gotten used to goals, plans, and making shit happen. So, I dealt with it the same way I did a lot of things now -- I just locked it away and kept going. I didn't like spending my time thinking about the old days because memories are a bitch, too. I got up and began walking again with only one working boot heel. Hell, some days everything was a bitch.

I may have been sitting, but I had sat next to a clump of grass. Always look for concealment, despite how piss poor it was. Grass grew here in clumps that stuck out of the sand like a mistake. Nothing like the real grass like I had spent most of my life walking on. The bushes were runty mistakes, too. The only thing they had going for them was they burned easy.

I was in the high desert somewhere north of the town of Page if I'd done my route right, just inside what had once been Northern Arizona according to the tattered paper map I had left Salt Lake city with a while back. I scanned the sky. I always scanned the sky, walking or sitting, even though there was no real reason to out here. I was looking for the glint, the shadow, the feel of evil.

We had a guy with us somewhere back in the beginning who said his old unit's motto was "Death from Above." Most of us thought he meant he was a drone jockey. He hated that, and I grew to really dislike his rants about the difference and how special by implication he was. He wasn't. He died like all the rest. Fucking drones don't care how well you were trained or what a bad-ass you were. They killed you as dead as a fourteen year-old kid who didn't know his left from his right for shit who was given a gun, a half-assed uniform, and led into a skirmish with professionals.

I liked this part of the world, even though it was as alien as the moon compared to where I had started from. You could see a hundred miles in any direction, and the air had a clarity that still amazed me. Somewhere due west of me a patch of clouds were raining on some piece of lucky dirt. Over me, the sky was blue, cloudless, and had been for days. I was moving again, but I didn't feel enthusiastic about it. More and more I just didn't give a shit. Not caring was something that had plagued me on and off for years now. I probably should be trying to analyze why and fix it. Not giving a shit was no way to go through life in the best of times, and today was years down the road from those times. Once in a while I had thought it would turn around, that life would be, maybe not better for me, but better for the world around me. People had tried, hell, I had fought with them more than a few times for it. But in the end, we always lost. The wheel had turned, and what was once was never going to be again.

I had made a career out of not caring and taking insane risks for the sheer joy of it. I had never put much of a value on anyone's life except for mine and the few people I cared about. Now even that was slipping away, and had been for a while. I was losing it, and I didn't care. I had fought it for a long time, but I was tired. Really tired. Every once in a while a part of me screamed, *"You're losing your edge!"* My response? A mental shrug. Nevertheless, I kept going through the motions. I had to eat. I still liked to get laid once in a while. Hell, I needed to resupply. My shit was getting ragged from the boots up.

Somewhere ahead of me, just outside of Page, was a bus stop. People called them "bus stops", but I wouldn't be surprised to see a stagecoach made from the shell of a minivan pull up. Eventually, maybe in a week, I would be in Flagstaff, where the call had gone out that there was a need for people like me. Someone needed killers to put out or start fires in yet another pointless border skirmish between yet another set of wannabe warlords. My recruiter in Utah, a young believer, had wanted to give me the details about how the side that was going to hire me was the righteous one. I laughed in her face and told her, "Don't worry about it. I don't." She had recoiled from me like I had struck her. Her partner, and old vet, well, he just looked at me and smiled. He knew. Their crusade, her cause, whatever label you wanted to use, it was just another job in a long string of them for people like me. She would learn. I didn't want her to, but she would. Of that I had no doubt. If she lived long enough.

I got moving. Well, half-assed hobbling was more like it. My leg and thigh, the one that had taken one too many deep penetration wounds, was numb all the way down to the knee, which wasn't helping. I made it to the top of the sandstone ridge after a couple of awkward hops from rock to rock. Awkward because I had seen a snake trail in the sand just before I began hopping and I was trying to be careful about where I put my feet. My final jump had startled a horny toad, whose quick movement had upset my timing by a hair. It was far from a graceful and quiet movement, another reminder, as if I needed one, that what was once taken for granted had now become difficult.

I hadn't lost it completely. A young Navajo was sitting on a chunk of sandstone outcropping watching his handful of sheep graze about a hundred paces away from him. His bicycle was leaning against the same rock, and his rifle was in its sheath across the handle bars. I grinned and yelled, "*Yatahai!*" To say he was startled would be an understatement. He literally fell off of his seat and sprawled in the dirt. His dogs, two mixed breed collie types out tending the sheep, heard me and came hauling ass toward him. I saw him look to his bike and the rifle. I shook my head, smiled, held up one hand in greeting, and said, "hello," again in Navajo. He gave me a tentative smile with a hint of embarrassment. I told him in English, "Sorry about that. I would have yelled out if I knew you were here." He yelled something in Navajo at his dogs, who were standing off ten paces from me and barking their heads off.

"You okay with me coming closer? I just want to talk." He looked a little dubious but nodded his head and told me, "Come on. I'll make the dogs behave."

I almost laughed at that, but if it made him feel safer I was okay with it. I had already run it in my head. Him and his two dogs had a lifespan of maybe one second after I drew my guns. He wasn't looking all that reassured by my comment, but he still told me, "Sure," and settled back down on his rock after yelling at the dogs to get back on the job. The sheep? It was a nonevent as far as they were concerned. I settled down about ten paces from him on a conveniently chair- shaped rock. I kept his bike between us. No need in making him any more nervous than he already was. "So, how's the sheep ranching working out?" I asked him. He laughed and told me,

"It's the family business," and shrugged. For a second the thought that he might not want to have a conversation flashed through my head. It wasn't reality. The kid wanted to talk. He was seriously lonely. That was okay with me. I needed data.

"How did you get here? Are there more of you? Do you have a horse? You got some nice gear! Where did you get it? Is that body armor?"

I sighed. I hated having multiple questions slung at me like that. "You got a name?"

"Oh, yeah. I'm Al. Al Tsingine. That's short for Alfred. It was my grandfather's name."

Damn. This kid was a puppy. I told him, "That was a lot of questions, Al. You have any water?" He blinked and smiled. The kid was a smiler, but his people generally were, I had found.

"Ah, sure. Sorry. I've been out here for seven days and …"

He didn't finish it. He didn't need to finish. I was supposed to understand what he was telling me. I could have answered, "Yeah? I've been out here for twelve days by myself, and I have enjoyed it. Well, yesterday I got horny. But other than that, I don't have a problem with it." I didn't. He didn't need to know. Plus, I wanted to keep him talking, and getting him weirded out wouldn't help.

He passed me a ceramic jug that had been fitted into a woven wool sock. I pulled the carved pine cork out and took a deep pull after weighing it first in my hand. I drank deep, he had plenty, but sucking down all his water would have been bad manners. I was a lot of things, but I tried to avoid being an asshole whenever possible. It was difficult. I had been told a few times that I came by it naturally, but I liked to think that I tried not to be.

The water was cool and actually tasted good. Both were pleasant surprises. I handed it back to him. He weighed it in his hand without being too obvious about it, did some calculations, and asked me if I wanted another drink. Once upon a time I would have declined. This wasn't then, and I was thirsty. I took another deep pour and handed it back. He didn't ask again. "Okay. I'm good." I wiped my mouth with the back of my hand and started answering his questions.

"I'm coming from Kanab. I was on a bike... I was taking the old highway, and hit a hole wrong about five miles out of town. I've been walking since." I didn't bother to add that I went through Kanab at night and my starting point had been a bit further north.

He didn't leave but a half of a second between my end and his start. "My cousin Alicia, she lives there. She works at the Saint's fort in the supply department. She says it's a great job. Sometimes she comes home and brings really good stuff like canned pineapple. Have you ever had that?" He took a breath and I got inside the conversational curve by asking him, "There is supposed to be a bus stop outside of Page. How far am I from it?"

"Oh, yeah. The toll place?"

"Yeah."

"About two miles that way," he pointed east and said, "Just keep the mountain in front of you. You can't miss it."

You couldn't miss the mountain. It filled the horizon in the direction he had pointed. I wasn't so sure about the, "Can't miss it" part, but it was good to know I was close.

"You sure got a lot of guns. Is that real body armor? Are you a contractor? They said a really famous contractor was coming this way. Maybe you might know him. His name is..."

"Al. Work with me here. Not so many questions at the same time."

He actually looked embarrassed when he told me, "Sorry..."

"No problem. Yeah, it's real body armor. No, I'm not a contractor. I'm doing my two year mission and I lost my name tag and partner a while ago."

He didn't look like he totally believed the last part. Maybe half of it. Damn, somebody let this kid run around by himself? I knew why he thought that. First off, I was a contractor. Once upon a time I would have been called an operator. The Feds had tainted that label. Second, well, I was probably one of the best armed men in the state. I usually was, no matter where I was.

I was wearing ceramic plate armor sewn inside a custom made canvas vest that I had lined with cotton except for the slits. I had cut slits in it to allow enough air to circulate for me to be semi-cool. I had thought it was a pretty good idea at the time, but it didn't make any difference that I had noticed. It did allow me to reach through and scratch myself a lot easier, so it wasn't a totally stupid idea.

My belt was held up by a leather Y-rig, with a fighting knife and two leather pouches attached to it and a scabbard fitted to ride along the back that once had held a sword. Now it carried a Winchester 30-30. My tooled leather gun belt was hung with two holsters, each filled with a Ruger .357, and a pouch with two spare cylinders for the Navy Colt I kept tucked in the gun belt, which was modified with a loop for the barrel to slide through to help me keep it in place. My cartridge loops were empty. I didn't like the brass sparkling in the sun. They would dull fast enough in the weather I spent most of my time in, but I had tracked a group once because they liked the old-school pistolero look too much. A K-98 bayonet hung just behind my left side Ruger, and I had a .38 snubbie in my boot.

I was a walking gun store. They were all well worn now. I'd had them for a long time. My hardware, which had once been considered stupidly retro, was now state-of-the-art, well, almost, and if I decided to sell it all I could afford to buy a farm. But I wasn't planning on selling them.

# Chapter Two

I said goodbye to Al after thirty minutes of conversation. He wanted me to stay around for dinner, but that was enough human company for the day. I took off, and after about fifteen minutes I stopped and waited to see if anyone was following me. Yeah, I was paranoid but I had earned the right.

I figured after I made it into Page I could see if they had someone who could fix my boots, get something to eat, and then come back and catch another ride to Flagstaff. I might not even have to come back. The odds were pretty good they stopped in town, too. I was looking good as far as making it to Flag on time, and if Page looked interesting and had a good Mex restaurant I might hole up there for a few days. It all depended on what was running south and how fast it got there. Nowadays you never knew for certain what was being used for mass transportation. If I got jammed up, I could always get word to my new employer. Wannabe warlords, if they could afford me, could usually afford the goodies that came with running a kingdom.

The two Navajos I had traded my bike to after it broke down had told me Page was worth stopping at. I didn't get much for the bike, but I was bargaining from a position that was one step up from nonexistent. At one point during our negotiations one of them told me, "Hey man, it's not like that bike is going anywhere, but you will, eventually." My reply? "You want to watch me toss it off the side of that ridge over there? Then maybe drop some rocks on it?" They didn't have any problem believing I would do it, either. I think it may have also crossed their minds that I was extremely well armed

9

and we were out in the middle of nowhere. I ended up with enough water for two days and a pound of corn flour. I was happy. They were happy. It was one of my few win-win encounters. I kind of liked it, but I didn't expect another one for at least five years.

I approached the way station from the back. Before I started down the dirt road to it I glassed it from the hill behind it. A hill that was crowned by a dried up pond that still had a wooden diving board sticking out of one side of the hill and as useless every hard-on I had for the past six months. Willows grew around it and a few cattle skulls and bones littered the dry ground. Below it, maybe six hundred paces, was a corral, then four houses and a trailer. Leading from them was an asphalt road that was not in the best of shape. The road led down the hill to an ancient trailer and a small wooden building. A horse was tied to a rail in front, and that was the toll booth and bus station. Off to the right, sitting on a low plateau and maybe eight miles away, was the town of Page.

In between here and there was the Colorado River, the aging but intact bridge over it, and the ruined hulk of the Glen Canyon Dam. The lake behind the dam still had some water. Getting to it, though, looked like a real bitch. The water was one reason there was still a town. It, and the bridge across the Colorado. Once upon a time the Navajo Electricity Generating Plant had been a big deal. I had been told in Salt Lake that the Saints were seriously considering cutting a deal with the Navajo Nation and doing a joint project to bring it back online, at least partially. It was an ugly looking plant, and those three stacks must have done wonders for the air quality when they were running full tilt.

I skirted the edge of the houses. I had no desire to catch a round because someone found me threatening. I did, with great difficulty, restrain my self from stomping a small mixed breed dog who dogged me for all but the last one hundred paces, yapping mindlessly and shrilly. A young man came out of the house on my left and watched me walk on by. He didn't seem friendly, but he never pointed the AK he was carrying at me, either. I waved, he scowled, and the fucking dog continued to yip. When I crossed the cattle guard at the bottom of the hill I flipped Yippy the dog off, paused to check out the view again, and get a feel for the place. Nothing felt off, so I climbed the wooden stairs into the "office" and stepped inside.

I wished I hadn't almost immediately. It was hotter than Hell inside that metal box. The guy on duty was behind a wooden desk, his feet up on it, and he was sound asleep. I mulled over evil ways to wake him up, starting with kicking his feet off the desk, but I quickly disregarded that one because I was afraid my boot would fall apart even more, if that was possible. I ran through a couple more, decided the Hell with it, sat down in the chair in front of his desk, and shouted, "Hey, sleepyhead!" Unfortunately, he didn't fall out of his chair. I regretted not busting a cap or pulling the desk out from under him. His, "Oh shit!" and his look of fear wasn't bad, but it was thin gruel to what could have been. He shouted back, "Who the Hell are you?!" I just stared at him. His bluster and anger drained out of him in about three beats. In a completely different tone of voice he asked me, "Can I help you sir?"

"Any chance I can get a ride into town?"

He laughed. As answers go, I find that laughter for a reply is never a good sign. I waited until he stopped. It wasn't long. He mumbled, "Mmmmm...yeah. Next convoy isn't due through here until tomorrow." He looked me over and added, "No offense, mister, but if we get regular people passing through they ain't going to be to eager to let you climb in with them." That made sense.

"No bus or cart service?"

"No. Been talk that one might be starting up, but as usual its been nothing but talk. Going to be kind of hard to do since the road gets real bad in places once you get twenty miles or so north of Kanab. How did you get here?"

"Took the old Kanab road until my bike busted a fork."

"No shit. Did..." He didn't get to finish. The same door I had come in busted open and the same scowl faced young man I had passed earlier rushed into the room. He barely made it a step into the room before I was back on my feet, both guns drawn and cocked, one pointed at sleepyhead, the other at him. Two things saved his life. The AK was at port arms and he yelled "Dad!" as he came through the door. He froze in place when he saw me. We all did. Sleepyhead handled it better than I expected.

He told the kid, "Damn it, Jacob! I hope you remembered to feed the cat." Jacob relaxed. I didn't. I told him, "Jacob. Go tell your backup it's okay." He looked at his dad who nodded and then he yelled out the door, "We got a cat!" Now I understood. Safe words and phrases.

I asked him, "So what was the kill word?"

He replied, "Dog."

"That's catchy."

He didn't smile. I was getting the feeling he didn't like me. Some people were like that. I just had to enter a room and it was all downhill for them.

12

Sleepyhead Dad sensed it, too, and said, "Son, did you see that? The man knows how to handle them guns."

"I saw it. I saw him come walking by the house, too. Came out of nowhere."

The trailer door hung open and a tow-headed kid of sixteen was staring in at me. He had a pump action shotgun hanging low and loose in his hand. He looked okay. Too bad he was going to have to go first if his friend kept pushing. Looking at the kid made me realize how old I was getting. America, or what passed for it now, had two big age groups for the most part. My generation, the generation young enough to survive the big die off after PowerDown, which had killed most of the real young, the out of shape middles, the fat and medicated, and the old. The second group was all the survivors' kids were of age or coming into it.

I decided to end the bullshit. I didn't want to be standing around in this sweat box chatting all day. "Jacob. You got a vehicle that runs?"

"Why?"

What a surly fuck, I thought. "Because I'll pay you to run me into town. That's why."

We began negotiating the price for my ride. After he realized I didn't want to buy his truck and I listened to them bitch about how much gas was we negotiated a price in silver. They wanted it up front and were surprised when I agreed to that. So I told them, "You look like decent, law-abiding young men." Then I lowered my voice and added, "I'll make sure I mention this when I report to Salt Lake."

Those two words changed everything. It was a guess on my part, but not a wild one. Even if they weren't Saints, they would be well aware of their presence and influence this close to the end of the Navaho Nation border. Inside of those two words was another possibility; I had just popped out of nowhere. I had admitted to coming from Kanab. I was heavily armed. Could I be a Danite hit man? Sleepyhead and his crew processed all of this and he seemed to like it, a lot.

He called an impromptu family conference. They walked away far enough that they thought I couldn't hear them. They were almost right. My hearing, once on pare with a wild animal, had declined a lot over the years. Too many loud blasts in tight spaces will do that. I heard enough to confirm that I had guessed correctly. My body armor hadn't gone unnoticed. Sleepyhead Dad told them, "That's got to be ceramic body armor! Nobody has that anymore but the rich..." here he lowered his voice, "and the Danites."

The Danites were the action arm of the Saints, the equivalent of the old Mossad. They were a strange bunch, fanatics, with the usual total commitment to killing enemies of the church, mixed with good manners, and a shit load of kids. I liked them and had worked with them before. They totally hated the Federal government, and that was even before everything fell apart.

They broke from the huddle, and everything was now sunshine and smiles. Well, almost. Jacob still wasn't a hundred percent in love with me yet. I figured there was a back story there, and I hoped I would not have to listen to it. Hell, if he gave me a few hints I could probably write it for him. He probably felt like it was a big deal. It was for him, but it wasn't unique. No way it could be. Not for someone like me.

Of course, we couldn't leave right away. He had to go back up the hill to get the truck, and Dad told him to check with Rebekah and see what she needed from town, and if any errands needed to be run. I was paying for an off-schedule town run for them it sounded like. I killed time talking to Sleepyhead Dad. "You got anyplace you'd recommend for me to stay at in town?" He ran down his list, all two of them, one of them sounded like a flophouse, the other was where visiting VIP's stayed. Then slyly, for him I'm sure, he suggested I go see the local Bishop and see if a good family could put me up. I pretended to think about that for a couple beats and then told him, "Naw. I want to keep a low profile."

"You here on business?"

Yes, he was a sly dog. I winked at him, "Nope. Just passing through."

He seemed disappointed. "Oh. Thought you might be here because of them Fed boys that just got in town. That," and here he looked troubled, "and word is the Apache might be coming this way."

Both were news to me, but it wouldn't do to let him know that. "Naw. I figure your people can throw them off the bridge just as well as I can." We all found that pretty damn funny, including the tow-headed kid who had been hanging on every word.

# Chapter Three

We rode into town in Jacob's Ford F150. It was what I expected. Old, immaculate, and modified in all the usual ways. No glass in the windows. Instead, he had the standard shield fitted to sit on top of the hood until manually raised. The shield was reinforced with steel and a slit for a view port. The back window had been replaced by a permanent window of the same type. The side windows were gone. He needed new tires and probably had for a couple years. He may have called it "his" truck, but my guess was it was "The Truck" for everyone living up on that hill.

I had seen a different set of tire tracks coming down the dirt road and passed a vehicle under a tarp sitting in the last house's carport. Probably a dune buggy from the shape, and used for patrolling and hunting. I hadn't cut any deer sign, so I wasn't sure what they could be eating. Probably making deals with the herdsmen for mutton or hunting wild beef or horses.

I was wondering where the choke point for toll enforcement and security was, because that trailer sure as hell didn't qualify. I had expected something at the bridge, it was easier to defend and control. I was right. I liked being right, and so far today I had been on a roll. Well, the day was still early, and the night was long.

It wasn't far to the bridge, and I was glad. If it had been

any further, I would have had Jacob stop the truck and switched places with the kid in the back. Jacob was trying to get me to talk by asking questions about Salt Lake, and I really didn't feel like answering them. We both agreed that the Tabernacle was worth going to see and hear. Thankfully, that got us to the bridge. We were waved through after Jacob chatted briefly with the young Navaho who came out to take a look at us. I noticed we didn't pay anything, either. We were waved through and proceeded slowly through a serpentine course designed to get us dead if the need arose.

I looked around while we rolled slowly forward and was impressed. The entrance had a decent size building at the bridge head. It had probably once been the visitor's center. It was surrounded by a round-shaped sandstone hill that had been gouged deeply to run the road through it. The hill, I found out later the locals called it Beehive mountain, had more than the usual number of shallow caves with some being used for heavy weapons emplacements. There were more than a few sandbag emplacements, too. Not a surprise as sand was not too hard to find around here. It looked to be all Navajo on duty, too. I found out later the Beehive was once considered a sacred mountain by them. As usual, that hadn't stopped progress.

Rolling across the bridge let me take a good look at the leftovers from the time before everything went to hell. The Glen Canyon Dam, a giant-sized progressive dump of concrete in the middle of one of the most beautiful places in the world. A feat of world class engineering, built in the wrong place and anchored by sandstone- natures version of frozen sand drifts. The dam had failed not long after PowerDown rather spectacularly. Enough debris was still in place to keep a much smaller Lake Powell filled with runoff and in time I suppose the water-stained sandstone left behind would be scoured clean. It still pissed me off to look at it. The only thing uglier was the coal-fired generating plant, which should have been

17

blown up the day after Powerdown. Why where these ugly pieces of shit built? To generate electricity for cities that never should have been built in the first place. PowerDown had taken care of the cities, especially in the southwest, which had already sucked down or polluted the aquifers that kept them alive. Changing weather and the resulting drought that never seemed to go away made sure that the survivors of PowerDown who wanted to continue to survive migrated the hell away.

I had them drop me at the town park and point me in the direction of where the cheap motels were, which they did after warning me that there were some strange people living in the old ones and I would be best off going with the ones they recommended. They also added the manager was a "Saint" and he would take care of me. I knew he had to be either that, or family, as people always steered business to whoever else was in their tribe, religion, or were related to them.

I had gone with the non VIP choice. My choice was called the Red Rock and it was just one of a handful of ancient motels all stuck in a motel ghetto. The difference between the Red Rock and the rest was it was still in "official" operation. The others? No one who wasn't drunk, high, or looking to get one or the other would even want to climb through one of the kicked in windows or doors and seek shelter inside of them. I found later a couple of them were actually livable depending how you defined "livable." The rest? I'm sure it was done, and I'm sure it wasn't something you could do very many times and survive. Hell, if it wasn't the trolls and ghouls that lived in them, it was the bugs. Just thinking about the odds of a scorpion bite made me shudder. I hated the evil little fuckers. They were the West's version of the water moccasin. Always pissed off and ready to mess with you just because they could. When I first came out this way I thought it would be rattlesnakes. I went two years without seeing a rattlesnake. I shook a scorpion out my boot the second night I crossed into what was once Atlzan, once the American Southwest, and now a collection of half-assed autonomous regions and American Indian Nations sprinkled with religious leader compounds, white only clans, and a lot of sun baked, half-starved feral whatevers, who were just one step up from wild dog packs and wouldn't turn down the roasted haunch of an unlucky traveler.

The Feds had pulled out of most of the American southwest after fighting a long ugly insurgency throughout most of the region that sputtered along, even after PowerDown. Even now they still tried protecting areas with resources and the related infrastructure, especially transportation, with mixed success. Lately they had been making noises about reunification of all the areas into one big, glorious USA again. Too bad they had screwed that up so badly the first few times they had tried. From what I heard, they were having problems holding on to what they had.

There was another power bloc that was growing and expanding steadily in the north. Even the Saints were looking over their shoulders and wondering about their borders. So far the Northerners had been content to raid to the east and expand into the heartland. They had a serious dislike of the Feds and were beginning to push them hard. Real hard. I made myself stop thinking about them. Nothing good lay there for me, and hadn't for a long time. I knew I was still welcome, hell, I was a legend, but I had left the north and never looked back. Instead, I waged my own personal war against the Feds. Eventually the fire inside me, that drove me, burned out, and I found myself at a loss. Hunted by the Feds, I had taken refuge with the Saints. I made myself useful to them and was paid well for it. Inside the Saints' borders the Feds had left me alone, except for the occasional assassination attempt, and at times I even convinced myself that I was happy.

They were good people, and inside their boundaries I could almost forget the people I had known and all the blood that been spilled. Sometimes I wore no gear at all when I went out, nothing but a single holster, everything else hung on their hooks inside my bedroom closet.

I wasn't happy. If anything, once the fire had died I found more and more I was left with the blackness. I quit taking jobs, and that didn't make a difference. I took jobs, and that didn't make a difference, either. The last one I did I had barely made it through to the end. Not because the people I was sent to talk to were any good. Rather, it was me. I just didn't care. It was the same old shit happening, with the same old people, and the results were always the same. The last job I had, for a tiny bit of time, not drawn my weapons. Muscle memory took over just in time. It helped he wasn't as good as he thought he was, but for a blink I didn't care. Even I knew that was not a good sign.

I walked the streets around the motel before I actually approached it. I wanted to know my exits and entrances, possible enemies, and mostly just to feel the flow of the place. It wasn't too hot, but I was aware of the sun. Lately I had found sun spots on my arms, and I had a nice one below my left ear. Crusty reminders that genetics had designed me for a land under a milder light. Also, a reminder, if I needed one, that I was no longer the young man I was when I had first strapped on my guns.

The town layout was based on a grid. Almost all these small towns were, and that worked for me on a number of levels. Mainly because once I got a feel for the layout, I had most of the possible city movement patterns locked in. Page didn't have much potential for a protracted street fighting battleground. No connected buildings or narrow alleys. That would make movement tough for any defenders, and easier for the raiders to isolate townspeople and burn or mortar out.

There had to be some kind of town perimeter guard or patrol, but I hadn't seen any sign of one. They were relying on picking them up far enough off to bug out to the shelter of one of the bridgeheads and hold until a Saints or Navajo nation react force showed up. Not really a plan, but better than nothing. My guess was it had been a long time since anyone had worried about raiders here.

I followed the faded sign to the office so I could check into my room. The clerk, probably the owner, was a white male in his early fifties who was sitting in an old metal folding chair outside the office door. He wasn't reading or talking to anyone. He was just staring off into yesterday probably, and waiting for something to happen, or the day to end. Instead, he got me. Check-in was easy. No questions asked by either of us other than wanting to know how long I wanted to pay for and how much. He was curious, but not curious enough to ask, which was not that unusual. Our conversation was brief.

"How much?"

"You want deluxe?"

"What do I get?"

"Stove works, probably. Well, one burner does...sometimes. You can come by and use my Internet if it's working. If we have power, which we do sometimes, your room a/c might work."

" A lot of mights and maybes in there for paying extra."

He shrugged. "Not going to lie. Everything we got was already old before PowerDown. It runs or it doesn't. The special gets you the room where last time I checked everything ran."

"I'll take it."

"Yes sir!"

Manners had improved greatly since PowerDown. Not surprising, as the survivors included a fair amount of angry, armed, and usually traumatized people who were as stable as old-school dynamite had been. I would like to think I added to that, as I believed bad manners was a borderline capitol crime, depending on who was involved and what my mood was like that day.

The room was just that - a room. It had the original kitchen appliances from the last renovation done, probably in 2005. The refrigerator had been duct taped shut twenty years ago at least, and someone had scrawled "Don't open!" with a black marker on the door. Of course, someone had opened it. The tape had been nicely slit by whoever it was. I couldn't smell dead refrigerator, so it had to have been a while ago. The bed was lumpy, and the linen looked old but clean. It better be. If I came down with bedbugs I was going to be very unhappy. So would the man who checked me in.

I threw my backpack on the bed, looked around, and sighed. It was a dump. For the average twenty year-old out there it would have been great. They would have no standard of comparison with what had once been, because the once-upon-a-time I knew no longer existed. For them, the a/c, which was actually running, and the light switch that worked would have been storybook. I shed some more gear, keeping the guns and sharp stabbing tools. I was going to leave the rifle, but I decided to keep it with me. The pack, which was essentially disposable, I left on the bed. My back ached from toting all this stuff, especially with my raggedy-ass boots making me walk funny.

I decided to see if I could find a cobbler right now. Then, get something to eat and see what else was for sale that was on my list. Salt should be easy enough to find. My ammo supply was fine, and I didn't plan on stocking up until it went on my new employers account.  As I walked out the door the electricity in my room died.

## Chapter Four

I found a cobbler without any difficulty. It was run by a wizened old white woman who ran the counter in front while her man operated a foot-powered sewing machine in the back. The shop smelled good- a mixture of leather and old feet. A smell I found comforting. I pulled my boots off. My foot wraps were less than pretty. I was glad she couldn't see them. Hell, I didn't want to look at them myself. It was hard to find socks for a long time, and I had gotten used to wrapping my feet in cloth squares as a substitute. I dropped the boots on the counter and handed her the boot heel. She set the heel down on top of the counter and moved it next to the boots with the tip of her index finger. She looked at my boots, looked at me, looked back at the boots, and yelled, "Hey, Bobby. Come check these out!"

"What?"

"Come here!"

He turned his head to look at us and made a frowny face. That's when I saw he had lost an eye somewhere along the line, and covered the missing socket with a black patch that he, or someone, had embroidered an eye onto. I liked it, and decided if I ever lost an eye I would do the same thing. Maybe with a skull for the pupil. I was thinking, *if I could wear one and cut a slit so I could see it might give me an added edge*, while he shuffled over to join us. She indicated my boots and told him, "He wants them resoled."

Bobby picked up the worst one up, turned it upside down, then stuck his finger through the hole by the toe, shook his head, and set it back down. "Mister, it would be cheaper for me to make you a new pair. I mean..."

I cut him off. I was trying to stay calm, but I was getting angry. I was telling myself, *"It's the truth. Don't get mad at him."* And I wasn't really mad at him. I was just mad. Mad that everything was slipping away. Mad that I was here. Mad that my life was what it was. "No. I want them fixed."

I think my expression had changed, or maybe it was the tone of my voice. Maybe both. He physically stepped back from me. The woman? She cocked her head, looked at me for a couple of beats, and asked, "They magic boots, sweetie?" I looked at her. I felt the anger spiking. If she was being a smartass or just fucking with me, I was going to make her extremely sorry. *"Burn down the fucking shop with them in it!"* flashed through my head. She didn't flinch. She just looked me in the eyes, and I realized she understood. The anger drained away as fast as it had arrived to be replaced with a sad weariness. "Yeah. They are." She nodded her head, and we all paused while she thought whatever she was thinking. My hope was she was thinking on how to fix them.

"Okay, how's this work for you: Bobby keeps the original uppers and redoes everything else?" I thought about it. It wasn't a bad idea. "Okay. How much? How long? And, do you have something in a size twelve I can wear until you get them done?" They had a pair that the guy had never came back for. Bobby told me, "It's been two years, and I'll have your boots done in three days. Odds are pretty slim he'll come back, and if he does, well, we'll find something else. You ruin them, then you pay for them."

"Sure."

I pulled them on. They were tight. "What size are these?"

"Eleven and a half," Bobby shrugged, "that's the best I got."

"It's okay, sweetie" the woman added. "You can walk from one end of this town to the other in five minutes." She had a point.

"Okay. Anyplace you can recommend to get something hot to eat and cold to drink?" Without hesitation she told me, "The Roadrunner. Make a left on the boulevard and you'll see it." Bobby didn't like that. "What about the Dock? Better crowd."

"Honey, does this man look like a rough crowd is a problem?"

She laughed. It was the raucous cry of a crow. For a second I felt a cold chill run down my spine. I looked closer at her. I got zero feeling from her. She had no presence. It hadn't set off any alarms because it wasn't a threat. Very strange. It was unique, but I had run across people like her before. Not often, and only back in the day. I didn't want to think about back in the day. I shut it down. If it wasn't a threat, then it wasn't a problem.

"You go have a bowl of chili at the Roadrunner. You'll like it."

"Thanks."

I walked out the door and made the left on the street, boulevard was a little to grand for what it was, which was just another pockmarked, sand-drifted, and faded excuse for a main street. I heard that damn crow laugh in my head until I found the Roadrunner. It didn't look like much from the outside. The walls were white painted cinder blocks originally; now it was white in places and gray where the paint had been sanded off by the wind. There was the support for a sign. The actual sign that it once had supported was gone, probably blown away. It didn't rain a lot around this part of the world, but the wind, it blew like the devils breath, hot, nasty, and for hours, until it made you crazy. Crazy as in crazy mean.

A roadrunner had been painted on the street side wall, underneath it crude black block letters spelled out ROADRUNNER. Somebody had shot at the roadrunner, and his head no longer looked quite right. This work of art looked newer then the original wall paint. My guess was it had been done no more than five years ago from the level of paint fade. About five paces from walking in the door I was hit with an invisible wall of wrongness. This was not a good place. Bad things had happened here, and bad men were inside. I smiled. This was my kind of place.

I walked in the door. It was a screen door with a metal one behind it that was propped open. I let it slam behind me. I liked the sound of screen doors slamming. It reminded me of old movies about other peoples' happy lives. I liked it so much, I kicked backward and popped it back open so I could hear it slam again. I stepped to my right and smiled as it banged shut again behind me. "Hey, now! Don't you love the sound of a screen door slamming?" I asked the other patrons who had interrupted their important conversations to stare at me. Nobody answered. The bartender looked at me and went back to drawing designs on the bar top with his finger and a puddle of beer.

It was almost the usual place with the usual people doing the same stupid shit. Almost. This place was different for two reasons. I instantly liked both of them. The first was the table full of bad-asses. Four males, two of them Indians, and not the Navajo type. Their faces were sharper, more angles than planes. They looked leaner, too, from what I could

27

see. Built for going the distance rather than working in one place all day. They would be quick.

Both of them were wearing leather holsters like mine, except theirs had more leather cut away in front so they could draw faster. They also were packing butcher knives in handmade leather sheathes. It was just getting better and better. They were sitting with two white guys who were too young to have seen Mad Max, but they had instinctively grasped the concept that looking like a B movie bad-ass would intimidate peace-loving citizens. The skull motif had been overdone when I was their age. Now it just said, "Trying too hard!" They were probably from what used to be California. The second reason was the barmaid. She was beautiful. Enough so that it distracted me from the staring contest I was having with the assholes at the table. I'm sure they thought they won, but I didn't care.

She came out of the back room and was carrying a fresh bottle of skullfuck, complete with worm, balanced on a little tray like this was actually someplace where people cared about presentation. She smiled at me, said, "Have a seat, stranger," and was past me in a hummingbird's heartbeat.

I watched her move. She had a great ass, and black hair long enough to caress the curves of it. I thought about how it would be nice to be that hair while I pulled up a seat at a table where I could keep my back against the wall and watch the doors. I nodded to the old guy lost in his drink a couple of tables down. He didn't even notice. I wasn't surprised. All bars like these had an old man or woman whose job was to stare into their drink and occasionally bust into tears or rants.

I watched as she dropped off the bottle, grimaced at their bullshit comments, and almost evaded an ass grope. She spun her way out of that one and told them to watch their hands. They laughed. As she made her way to me I watched them. One white guy was telling the other who wasn't listening because he was too busy watching her walk away, "I'm gonna get me some of that." He was an idiot. I was confirming my kill order and he was last on the list. His buddy was next. The Indians though, they were both good. Probably very good. That was unusual. People that good don't spend time in little towns like this, except to pass through. They went where the money was. Yet, here we were. One was tilted back in his chair, staring at the ceiling. The other Indian was looking at me. Not looking, appraising. He would be first. Our eyes locked. I knew him. He knew me. He gave me the lizard grin, thin-lipped and cold-blooded. I winked. Fuck him. The bar maid was almost to my table, so I focused on her. It was a pleasure. She looked as nice coming as she did going.

"What can I get you?"

"Is your bartender as worthless in a fight as I think he is?"

She looked over her shoulder quickly. When she looked back at me her face had tightened, "Yes, he is. He's got a 12-gauge under the bar, but I think he would rather use the back door first."

"Yeah. Okay. You got any iced tea?"

"Sun tea...not iced. That work?"

"Sugar?"

She smiled, "You mean for the tea?"

I felt it. It had been a long time. "Yeah, for the tea." Another big smile from her. I liked that smile.

"Coming right up," and she was gone. I didn't bother looking over at the assholes. I was running a new scenario through my head.

When she brought me my tea it was in a clear glass that was actually clean. She bent over to set it on the table, and I noticed that one more button had been loosened on her blouse. I liked the view.

"There you go." She didn't rush to stand up, either. I was okay with that. She smiled, straightened up slowly, and said, "Back to the assholes."

"Before you go..."

"Yeah?"

"Where exactly is that shotgun?"

"About a foot to his right. It's loaded with one in the chamber. Don't be messing up my floors. Unless it's..."

"Hey, baby. Bring that pretty ass over here!"

This was from the white guy who thought he was going to get some. He was, too. I was positive of that. "Those assholes." She yelled, "Hang on!" I heard her mutter, "The shit I gotta put up with to make a living." Then she was gone. I sat there nursing my tea and watching. They got drunker and nastier. The old man went to sleep. Two people came in, looked at the table of drunken assholes, and spun on their heels and bailed. When she came by to freshen up my drink I asked her, "You have a name?"

"Kat."

"I like it. You look like one." She did, too. Or an elf-girl. "Move like one, too," I added.

"Thanks. How about you?"

"I don't have a name anymore."

"Really?"

"Yep."

"So, should I call you Unknown or No-name?"

"Yeah."

She laughed. "Okay, Unknown. I get off in two hours...think you can nurse that drink that long?"

"Oh, I think you'll be closing early."

"Hah! I should call you Dreamer instead."

I just smiled. I saw her eyes change for a second. They got harder, more focused. Then the Indian called for her. I had noticed they didn't like her spending more than a couple of sentences with me. I was going to have to fix that. I leaned back in my chair. It helped relieve the back pain I felt damn near every day I wore a pack now. My leg was tingling. A good sign, that. It meant it had not gone completely dead on me yet. One of these days it would not only stay numb, but start dying on me, if it wasn't already. The doctor I had seen told me eventually it would have to come off. That wasn't going to happen. No. Fucking. Way.

A loud scream of pain, and I refocused. Kat was yelling, "You cocksucker! That hurt!" while she rubbed her left breast. The assholes were laughing, all of them except for Lizard Lips, who just looked amused. It was show time. I decided to go with Plan B instead of the usual Plan A. Why? Because it was riskier. Riskier could be considered showing off, but more and more I found myself going with it instead of basing my actions on hard won experience.

I stood up and dropped a couple of silver dollars on the table top. Yeah, I was way over-tipping, but I wanted them to see the silver, hear it clink, and process what it meant. Out of the corner of my eye I noticed Lizard Lips shift position and drop his hand down to his side. For an Indian, he could hold his liquor better than most. I walked past them at the table and without looking at her I raised my hand and said, "Thanks. See you around." I had to walk past the bar to get out the door. About ten paces from the door I hesitated, turned to the dumbass barkeep who was now polishing glasses, and asked him, "Hey, you got any matches?" I took a step toward him and went into overdrive. I hit the bar, grabbed the edge, and threw myself over the top. In doing that I knocked the barkeep back against the bottles. I liked the sound that made.

The shotgun was where she said it was. Now came the fun part. Was it actually loaded, and hopefully not with bird shot, either? I had to flip it since it was facing the right direction for a right-hander, and I was left-handed. While did

31

this, I took an extra second to bounce the butt off the barkeep's forehead. He was yelling in my ear, "What the hell you doing?!" I didn't need any distractions, and it also was irritating. Then it was pump, watch the already loaded round eject, tuck it to my shoulder, and start acquiring targets. I still loved this part. Everything else had turned to stale, same-old-same-old, but this, this was magic. This was the rush drugs had always promised in the beginning and never came close to delivering after the first few times. Life was chopped into frames of clarity and beauty that in real time lasted microseconds, but crawled in this, the magic time, the time of killing.

I pulled the trigger and Lizard Lips went sideways. That happens when you are off balance and 7 or 8 balls about the size of a .38 bullet slap you all at once. He was good. Better than I thought. He still managed to draw and touch my right shoulder as he went down. I jacked the pump and found target two as I moved towards the end of the bar. He was just as good as his buddy. If I hadn't have moved, my head would have been all over the wall, but I had, and it was his head that got turned into a bunch of puzzle pieces.

I hit the waist-high swinging door at the end of the bar with the intention of coming out fast and hosing the two white boys down. I got through that, pivoted, and pushed off with my bad leg, except it wasn't where my head told me it was supposed to be. I lost my balance and went down hard. Not good. Not good at all. I was getting untangled and back on my feet knowing I had been too slow. Both of the white boys were up and moving towards me. One of them was screaming, in the lead, and had his butcher knife held low in his hand. The other one had his gun drawn, but couldn't shoot because his partners bull rush fouled his shooting lane. I had cleared and pumped a new shell, but when I pulled the trigger all I heard was click. Well, I hadn't asked her how many were loaded had I? Oh ,well.

I dropped the shotgun and went for what I should have started with, my Rugers, when he hit me and bounced us both back against the wall. He was snarling, "Fuck you," his eyes were glazed with drink, focusing only because of the adrenalin rush and the victory that was just seconds away. He wanted to be in close for the knife work, so I pulled him in even closer. *"Fine, you sonafabitch,"* I thought, and pulled my bayonet from its metal sheath, pulled him in tight with my right arm, and reached around with my left and punched the blade into his kidney. He stiffened and I shoved him back towards his partner. I needed the space to draw, and I was going to be cutting this one just a little too close.

That's when I heard the "boom" of a large bore handgun. It was followed by another one, and I watched the other white guy go down. I saw Kat, standing there in a two-handed shooters stance, holding a Ruger GP100 with a long fucking barrel.

"That's a big gun for a little woman."

"The world is filled with big assholes."

"Yeah. You got a point."

"You know you have a knife sticking out of your leg?" I looked down, pulled it out, dropped it, and said, "You wouldn't believe how many times people have fucked this leg up. You got any bandages?"

"Yeah. Let me get them."

I fished out the big wound bandage I carried in my pant legs pocket. It was one of the last of the old ones, and I had really hoped I would never have to use it, especially on myself. By then I was starting to get dizzy. I took the dressing, ripped open the packaging with my teeth and  pressed it against my upper leg hoping to stop most of the blood loss. Then I slowly slid down the wall and waited for her to return.

## Chapter Five

I came to on and off over the next few hours. At least, I think it was hours. I wasn't feeling a lot of pain, nothing bad enough to make me want to scream. What was putting me out was blood loss and maybe a touch of shock. The longest period of awareness was riding in the back of a pickup, the night was dark, the air cold, and the stars brilliant in the sky above. That period shook me because I kept fading out of now time to back then time. Back then was a long time ago, but now it seemed like I could touch it. I remember yelling for Max and Night, but I didn't get an answer. I felt Night close by, which was good enough. Hell, it was better then good. I went back to sleep smiling.

I woke up inside a beehive. At least that was what I thought it was at first. I found out later it was a hogan, a Navajo house made out of mud, railroad timbers, and wood. It smelled good inside. I always liked the smell of pine burning, even though it made for excellent chimney fires. Kat was there, as was a male Navajo who was looking at my leg.

"He's awake." This was from Kat. I replied, "Yes, he is." I thought it was moderately funny, but they didn't smile. The light was coming from a kerosene lamp that other than the fireplace, a converted fifty gallon drum, was the one source of light. It left shadows on their faces that made them harder to read than I liked.

The Navaho male introduced himself to me. It turned out that his name was Tyrone, which I thought was the funniest thing I had heard in years. Both Kat and Tyrone ended up shaking their heads and leaving me to lay there laughing and holding my side for a while until I calmed down. Tyrone was the town EMT and a former army medic. He wasn't gay, either. Not that I cared, though it was unusual in my experience. Kind of like a male antique store owner with five kids from three different women.

Our first conversation began with him looking at my leg and saying, "You got one seriously messed up leg and thigh, my friend. You even feel anything where he stabbed you?"

"No."

"Been that way for awhile?"

"Yeah."

"Seen a real doctor about it?"

"Yeah."

He looked at me. He wasn't a youngster, and I didn't need to ask him to know he had seen some shit in his day.

"So, you know?"

Kat was listening. Women are always listening. They can be doing three different things, including holding a conversation with a friend ,and still here everything that's said. I didn't feel like having a discussion about what I had been told with her there. Hell, I wasn't sure I wanted to tell Tyrone. He may be doing the kindly, caring health care professional routine, but it was really none of his business.

"I know that I should have shot all four of them assholes as soon as I came in the door." Then I went back to sleep.

I slept on and off, mostly on, for the next few days. The morning of the third day I decided to start my rehab, which meant walking further than the outhouse. I was not thrilled about doing it. I had been down leg rehab lane before and it was a bitch then. My guess was it was going to suck a billion times more now. A young body is far more forgiving of life's puncture wounds

The first thing I found out was my leg was almost completely dead from the thigh to the knee. Not completely, I could still get it to move, and it hadn't forgot how to hurt. It just felt wrong. Even the pain felt wrong. Most times there was barely anything, and then out of nowhere the wires made the right connection and it felt like multitudes of mice were inside my leg trying to cut their way out with tiny chainsaws. Even worse was I couldn't trust my leg. I wasn't sure it would plant or flex right, and a lot of my timing with my guns was tied to my legs working correctly. I had been compensating for the numbness for a while, and I had noticed that doing that helped, but not enough. I wasn't anywhere near as good as I was once. I was still good when everything worked right. The problem before was, I wasn't a hundred percent sure when it would shut down on me. Now I didn't have to worry. It had.

Once I started walking the only way to keep going without relying on the branch Grandma had found for me was by swinging it as best as I could. I no longer walked, I lurched. I was most unhappy about that. I also didn't get too far past the outhouse before I decided that this was a good enough start, but it was a better time to take a nap.

The next few weeks were interesting as me and Grandma put some serious quality time in together. More than I had put in with anyone who was a civilian in decades. Kat wasn't around much during this, as she was out running errands or whatever. Grandma wasn't too clear on it and Ty, as he preferred to be called, wasn't either. I saw her briefly here and there, but she spent most of it talking to Grandma in Navajo. She did manage to find time to update me on what was happening in the world, well, this section of it, anyway. What she told me was fascinating, especially when I put it together with the odds and ends of facts, rumors, and gossip I knew.

The world, which to me meant was used to be called the United States of America, was changing again. It would be more truthful to say it was evolving, and had been since the crash, but I didn't see it that way. To me, and the people my age, it was change, and as usual, it meant more pain and bloodshed. Normally I would have welcomed the news. Surfing change was what I did for a living. Hell, it was why I was on my way to Flagstaff. That pain and bloodshed usually needed professional guidance to be effective without destroying too much of what remained of the infrastructure. The other part to it was wherever you found destructive change you found assholes, and I liked removing them from this plain of existence. I was very good at that.

Kat had her serious face on as she talked to me. I didn't really know her well enough to read all her moods and expressions, but a woman wearing her serious face was an easy one. Even for me. I have to admit I was disappointed, but I knew if I wanted to get laid, or just a little oral stimulation, I was going to have to dig out my, "I'm here for you, baby. Please share with me," face. It was a little early for a "relationship" discussion, and I was really hoping she wasn't going to break the news to me about her monthly lip blister problem. Instead I heard, "We got problems." I raised an eyebrow and asked, "What kind of problems would that be?"

"We're being invaded."

I was tired, cranky, and I was never good about being patient. A couple of thoughts zipped through my head like, "She's a civilian", and "Sex". So, I mentally took a deep breath and resigned myself to having to work the situation report out of her.

"By who, when and where?"

She sighed. That told me it was going to take a while. I shifted my position and winced, not because I was feeling any pain, rather in hopes that it might motivate her to condense it, and checked my face muscles to make sure my listening face hadn't fallen off.

She scanned my face and must've liked what she saw because she told me, "I'll skip some of the background. You probably know it anyway. We're being invaded by Apaches. They want the bridge, the water, and the coal plant, worthless as that is." I cut in with, "Who, what, where, and why, Kat?"

"The why?" Here she frowned, she looked cute doing it, which was unusual in a woman because it usually was the first step in the escalation process. Frowns, to me, were the cracks in the ice and led to a lot of cold ugliness. She continued, "I think I got the 'what' with that too. The 'where' is obvious. The 'why' is where it gets fuzzy. That's one of the reasons I haven't been around much. The People are trying to figure out what to do, and I've been bouncing around to different Chapter Houses talking and listening. Plus, it was better to stay out of town for a while, anyway." She gave me a significant look.

"Yeah, Grandma told me. Some people got a bit riled up over the shooting."

"Nothing major. I'm *Dine* and this is our place. They weren't *Dine* so...." She shrugged, and added, "The Feds didn't have many friends here, and even less now. They left town about a week ago."

"So you're okay?"

"For now."

Left unspoken was the soon to arrive Apaches, who probably would want to talk to both of us for at least a minute or two before they began working on making us scream.

I asked her, "So what, or who, is sending them this way?"

"Yeah. That's important. There are a couple of theories, actually more, but I'll spare you the crazy shit and tell you the two I think are the closest to the truth. They are moving because they have to. You would think, especially listening to them, that they are the baddest people in the known universe. They are getting pushed hard by the Comanche who are, supposedly, even meaner, and have a lot more people. They are pushing the Apache because they saw how the *Lakota* prospered by expanding, and because they need water. Not many people are talking about it, but I think water is the real driver."

I interrupted her, "You realize that after the Apache will come the Comanche. They have to come this way. That part of the world is going dry. Hell, Texas can't support half the people left there much longer. There won't be as many dying as there was after PowerDown, but that won't matter to them because it will be just as ugly. My generation got to kill each other over the loss of air conditioning and light. Yours gets to carry on the tradition, except this time it's going to be all about water."

"Were you scared when the power went out? I mean, I heard stories about the big cities, you know, people eating each other..." Then she realized what she said and how old I was. "I'm sorry. I know that's a touchy subject."

I smiled. I didn't answer her right away. Not because I felt like leaving her hanging on a hook. No, it was because I was seeing people and places that I tried not to think about now. "No, Kat. I wasn't scared. I was too busy having a good time." She looked at me, and I could see the wheels turning as she processed that. I jammed them by asking her, "Is that everything?"

"No. Some think the Feds are behind the Apache moving. They want them to do their dirty work here because they have their own plans. Anyways, they are headed this way soon. We have maybe a couple of weeks to figure out what we're going to do and how to do it."

"What about the Saints?"

"We're trying to find out. I'm not counting on them. We have pretty good relations with them, but we don't know how much they're willing to commit to and what the price will be."

"How come you know so much, Kat?" I said it casually, but I meant it. Given a choice between sounding like an asshole or being setup, I always went with being an asshole.

"You mean for a barmaid?"

"Yeah."

"You aren't to subtle are you, Mr. Unknown."

I didn't answer. I waited for one.

She did. It took a minute, a minute were she tried staring me down. That didn't work. So, she told me. "I'm the daughter of a man who was important. My mother was an Anglo. She left and took me with her when I was little. I came back when I was older with my mother, but she lived off my Father with out living with him. I am accepted, but I am lost. I used to think of myself as a bridge between what was left of the Anglo world and the People." She shrugged and looked at me.

I knew now was my time to say something profound, something that would be a bond, a bridge between us. I couldn't think of anything, as usual. She waited, and after a few minutes she realized I wasn't going to say anything, let alone what she wanted to hear. She shook her head, said goodbye to Grandma, and left. I didn't move from where I was for a long time.

After Kat left company got scarce, and it was back to hanging with Grandma. She was old school, hell, she probably was alive the first time men walked around with revolvers in holsters. I wasn't going to ask if she was, as that probably

41

wasn't her idea of the golden age. I never quite got my tongue around her name, so I called her Grandma. She called me *Gaagii*. That shook me for more than a minute the first time she did. It sounded too close to what my friends had called me in another world. She saw it and patted me, and told me, "Okay. It's okay. I know." *"Know what?"* went through my head, but I got real tired again and went to sleep. When I woke up I wasn't sure if I had dreamed it or not. Grandma cleaned my wound, which even I could tell wasn't healing fast enough for what was coming. I had a fair amount of experience in wounds, both my own and other people's by now.

Grandma fed me a lot of corn, some of it was blue, which was pretty cool. I ate squash and I ate sheep. I think it was sheep. I didn't ask. I just ate. I am good at that. Even better was she liked feeding me. We got along, and she started talking to me more. Much to my surprise she spoke excellent English with the same sing song lilt to it that I had heard with other Navajos. It was still disconcerting, especially when she would call me *Gaagii,* but I got used to it. I asked her what that meant in *Dine.* I had been corrected gently by her to use that instead of Navajo, but all she did was smile and say, "That's your true name in our language." I let it go and filed it away to ask Kat. Hopefully it didn't translate as "shithead" or "Man with ugly face."

What I wanted to know from her most of all was when Kat was coming back? I was feeling better, and I missed her. I knew I wasn't going to Flagstaff. Not with my leg like this, and maybe never. I suppose I should have been worried about people looking for me. I wasn't. For me, it was another bar dustup. And if they did, so what? Even with a bad leg, I figured I could take who ever I ran into. I was even considering asking Kat if she wanted to go back to Utah with me. That is, if she ever talked to me again.

# Chapter Six

I started walking again, this time seriously, the day after Kat left. I chose as my workout route a trail that went all of sixty feet up to a sandstone ledge about two miles from the beehive. Once there, I would watch the clouds and their shadows race across the desert and let my mind idle. While I did that, I would pull off the bandage on my leg, expose it to the air, and tell myself it was healing. Once I saw a big ass bird with the wingspan and size of a drone fly over head. That gave me the cold sweats, until I figured out it was a condor. That put me in a bad mood for the rest of the day.

The next day I asked Grandma, "You call me *Gaagii,* but you won't tell me what it means. You told me 'you know', but you won't tell me what you know. Why?" I was trying to keep the anger out of my voice, and I thought I had until I saw her flinch. That me feel small and very much like an asshole. I added quietly, "I would appreciate it." Grandma looked away from me and continued smashing corn with what I had first taken for a dildo. Fortunately, I hadn't said what I had thought out loud. She stopped, set her pestle down, and said, "You're right. I apologize. I will tell you, but I don't want to discuss this again."

"Okay."

"Do you know any of our creation stories?"

"No."

"Good," then she laughed. She added quickly, "It will make it easier to explain because your name is one with certain connotations that I don't see. My vision is from that, but filtered by my life experiences. Do you understand?"

"You never told me what you did before PowerDown."

"I taught Shamanistic Practices of the Southwestern Indians at the University of Arizona in Flagstaff."

"I would never have guessed. You a Burner too?"

"No. I always thought of them as lost souls who decorated themselves with the shiny parts of other peoples' beliefs in hopes that it would transform them. Somewhat like the idea that buying a purse from a designer would transform you into a desirable object."

"Yeah. I remember that."

She looked at me and said, "You really didn't want to know all that did you?"

"Not really."

"Okay. Your name, *Gaagii,* translates to Raven. That is your clan. Your totem. Your spirit guide." She paused, then said, "It would help if you nodded as I tell you this. It makes it flow easier for me."

"Sure." I nodded. She gave me the look. I knew what that meant. I wasn't going to be getting any blue corn tonight if I didn't start acting right. That was okay. I've been hungry before, and probably will be again.

She sighed, probably mentally counted to ten, and continued, "I have visions. I saw you before you came." She paused, then said, "You scared me. No. What you represent scares me, and I never thought that it would."

I nodded. This was getting interesting. She gave me a smile of approval. The blue corn was back on.

"You walk the road and don't see it. I see it and I don't want to walk it. I'm sorry, I am being cryptic and that doesn't

45

answer your question.  What I know is that we both have journeys in front of us."

She gave me a significant look.  I nodded and told her, "Yeah.  I know.  It's a long way back to Salt Lake."  She didn't say anything in reply.  She looked at me and I saw the sadness cross her eyes.  She knew I saw it and looked away.  It was an awkward moment, so I asked her, "When do we eat?"  She whispered the answer, "Soon."


A few days later Ty showed up with Kat after sundown.  He had antibiotics, which he had bought with the money I had given him.  Kat had news.  She didn't look happy and neither did Ty, and that was before he looked at my leg.  They also seemed to have changed around me. They were distant.  More watchful.

"So, whats up, Kat?"

"Lots," was her reply.

Then we had to chit chat.  Well, they did.  Nobody here seemed to understand that getting to the point was the main purpose for talking, but I kept my tongue in check. Kat sat next to me and was very concerned about me. Especially about my leg after Ty took a look at it and then stuck me with the needle.  Looking at her in the flickering light of the lantern I remembered how much she excited me.  Especially when she leaned over to look at my leg and  I could smell the soap and woman smell radiating off her.

Right then I began to think of a subtle way of telling her that if she was spending the night I hoped it was next to me.  After a few minutes I gave up on subtle, leaned over, and whispered in her ear, "You spending the night?"  She tilted her head to look at me, her hair brushed my good leg,   and I felt young again.  She grinned, and said,"Yes."

"Good."  I reached over and let my hand curve across her leg while I leaned in even closer, and whispered, "Thanks."

Then I checked out Grandma and Ty's reaction. They seemed okay with it. Then Ty told me, " You stirred up some people, Gardener. More so than we originally thought. Killing Apaches always does. Killing a couple of Feds does, too. Killing them both at one time is like a grand slam." Kat added, "Especially when it's Gardener doing it. That changed everything." There was more than a little empty air time after that. I thought about denying it and decided not to. I was who I was. "So, who knows?" Ty answered, "Everyone."

"Is that like 'everyone' who is *Dine*? Or the entire town? Or just for forty miles in every direction?" I guess I sounded sharper than I thought, because they both looked taken aback. *Speaking in concise, fact-based sentences must not be taught around here*, I thought for the twentieth time. Kat told me, "Everyone. It will be in Flagstaff soon, if it isn't already."

"Tell me about the Feds, Kat."

"They said they were contractors here to provide security for a Fed survey team. The Nation wants to get the coal plant up and running again. The Feds would be providing the hardware, probably salvage from somewhere back east. Most think they were really part of an advance team for the Apaches."

"People keep telling me, 'The Apaches are coming! The Apaches are coming!' They make a wrong turn and end up in whatever the hell Texas is calling itself these days?"

Ty replied, "They're coming. Word is there was a skirmish between one of our patrols and one of theirs yesterday not far from here. I'm headed to the Beehive to work as a medic. The towns people were told to get across the bridge when the alarm goes off, or head back to their Chapter Houses. The Navajo Reserve has been called up, and they're already headed to the Bridge or Glen Canyon City where we plan to stop them before they get here."

"What do you have that can stop them?"

Ty blinked, and said, "You know. Guns and stuff. The usual." He was keeping his face way too deadpan. I knew that way back when the US Army had trained him as a medic and he had used his skills in Africa. I was sure he remembered enough to know that they were going to have to go bigger than that.

"If the Feds are involved, you might want to see what the Saints can bring to the party."

"I know. That's way over my pay grade."

Kat jumped in with, "You're Gardener! We should take you to see the Bridge Commander! You could take charge and we can really kick some ass!"

Now it was my turn to go with the stone face. It wasn't hard. That was the way I looked all the time, I've been told. "No, Kat. Too late. I don't do savior work anymore, and most of all I'm not in shape for it."

"So what are you going to do?" She asked me.

"I don't know." I didn't, either, and I wasn't worried about it.

"Yeah, Gardener...damn, I can't believe I'm talking to The Gardener. The Apaches will come looking for you. They hate your guts." Kat laughed and added, "Sure as hell won't be any bounty hunters." I grinned at that. "Yeah. They got discouraged."

There was a large bounty for anyone who delivered my head to the feds. They didn't say "Dead or alive." It was assumed the only way I would be showing up would be as a corpse. Ty laughed, "No kidding. You only killed, what, a small cities worth of them?" Kat added, "Hell, Ty, Gardener blew up a town full of them in one day!" I just smiled. It was half that number and only a few blocks, but having a rep was like carrying an extra Ruger. Ty continued, "And word went out from people up North that anyone who delivered you to the feds wouldn't live long enough to enjoy the money, nor would any family out to third cousins, the town they lived in, and their pets."

"Except for the dogs." I said this quietly.
Kat opened her mouth to say something, more than likely to ask about the dog exemption, but she saw the my face and changed her mind. I had gone inward. Back to places, and people, and a time. I cut it off. When I refocused they were both staring at me. I laughed, at least I think I did, and said, "I'm back."

I could feel a fever coming on and decided to get this conversation back on track and then go lie down. "So, if I don't have to worry about the feds, then that leaves the Indians. Why them?"

Ty told me, "Not just Indians, Gardener. Apaches."
"So what?"

"No. Not 'so what?'" Kat told me gently. "They are vindictive, and they will want to get some payback. Especially now."

"Why now?" I was curious.

"Because they know who you are."

"They have any shooters?"

Ty nodded, grimaced, and said, "You got their two best, but all of them are pretty good." Kat added, "They aren't above shooting you in the back or swarming you, either." I laughed. "So, I can count on your people to have my back?" They both looked at each. Kat looked down. Ty met my eyes and said, "I doubt it." I laughed and laughed. When I got over it I told them, "Yeah. I thought so."


When Ty left he took Grandma with him. They said something about sleeping under the stars. That was thoughtful. It wouldn't have stopped me from what I had in mind, but it was a pretty clear sign that I wouldn't have any problem getting to sleep later. She was gentle and I was restrained by my leg, so what happened was different than my usual use-them-and-loose-them encounter. Far different. I had never let myself be touched inside after that day, but she managed to get through to me, and in doing so I realized how empty and thirsty a part of me had become. I drank her caresses like a man who had spent far too long in the desert, and despite my fever I wanted more. I got it, too. When I woke up the next morning the hogan door was open for light, and she was propped up on one arm watching me.

"Hey."

"Hey to you" I told her. I smiled. I hadn't slept well, my dreams were not pretty, but that was not unusual and I was used to going without enough sleep. She didn't smile back. Instead she asked me, "You still miss her, don't you?" I blinked, not from surprise, rather from the sudden pain in my chest. Her words were an ice pick to my heart. She was the one who was surprised. The change in my attitude, my face, must have been clear enough. She sat up, a lovely sight at any other time but not now. "I'm sorry!' Did I ..."

She was frightened and genuinely worried. Intellectually I understood that, and I knew I was supposed to tell her it was okay. I also knew that I shouldn't be getting angry, but I was. I told her quietly, "Why don't you go." She didn't say a word as she dressed. I didn't look at her. She was no longer there for me. Instead, I pulled one of my pistols, opened the gate, and spun the cylinder around and around. She paused in the door. I suppose she was waiting for me to say something. I didn't. She left. Ten minutes later I walked outside into the sun, away from the hogan, fell to my knees, and screamed until my throat felt like it was bleeding.

I was still sitting there when Kat returned with Ty and Grandmother. They approached me cautiously, and when they were about ten paces from me they stopped and didn't say a word. I knew they were there, but I didn't say a word. Why? For two reasons, really: I was past thirsty, way past parched, and deep into the land where my throat tissue could polish pine. The other was I didn't care. In fact, I would have been happy if they all just went away after leaving me a gallon of water to drink. They went away.

Kat had tried to come closer but Grandmother had called her back. I sat out there until the sun began to go down, and I thought about a lot of things, but never one thought for more than a moment. I would touch them mentally and then recoil from the heat they generated. Some were as searing as the sun, while others just generated old pain like coals once the outer crust of memories crumbled away.

As the shadow cast from the butte in front of me began to darken, Kat came to me again. She stood there, on my right side, for about five minutes before she said, "I brought water." I stuck out my arm and beckoned for her to bring it. She placed it in my hand and I drained it and handed it back to her saying, "More." She came back with more, but this time stood a lot closer. I drained that, too, and wiped my mouth with the back of my hand. We waited together in the darkness for about five minutes before she spoke.

"You want to tell me what's going on?"

"No."

"I should have known better. She was as famous as you are once, and still is among the Northerners." I didn't say anything.

"So, what's next, Gardener?"

"I kill people. It's what I do." I went to stand up, and would have fallen over if she hadn't caught me. Once I got stabilized I stiff-armed her away from me, and bit back on what I wanted to say, which was, "Stay the fuck away from me!" I wasn't angry with her. I was angry with me. Angry with the way life had turned out. Angry with my leg. Angry that I still missed Night so much. I took a deep breath and said, "Sorry, my leg fell asleep."

"Oh. Okay. Do you need a hand?"

"No."

I stepped off and almost fell over again. I reached out, grabbed her shoulder, heard her wince, loosened my grip a little, and told her, "I'll take a shoulder instead, if you don't mind." We walked back slowly to the hogan where Ty was waiting. He pretended not to notice my difficulty walking, and I pretended not to notice that he had seen it.

"Gardener."

"Yeah, Ty."

"I talked to some people. They want to meet you and talk about what's going on."

"When's this supposed to happen?"

"How about now?"

# Chapter Seven

I thought about it. I wasn't doing anything else. Well, maybe apologizing to Kat eventually, and I had a pair of boots to pick up. Eventually, like in the next few days, I would be heading back to Salt Lake and killing Apaches, and whoever else got in the way. That was about it for a schedule. Somewhere in there was a vague desire to see if Kat wanted to go back to Utah with me. That might require some adjustments that I wasn't sure if I was up to and she was willing to put up with. "*No harm in asking,*" I thought. Plus, who knows. The meeting might be interesting as long as no one talked a lot and it was over fairly quickly. Maybe the women had made dessert.

"Sure. You coming, Kat?"

She looked surprised, and then said dryly, "Well, I was invited, but thanks for asking." I looked at Ty and we both started smiling about the same time. I told her, "Okay but I'm riding shotgun." I said goodbye to Grandmother. For a woman who always wore about six layers of clothes she was remarkably cool to touch. While I did that, Ty got my gear together and brought it to the truck. Grandma said something to Kat in *Dine*, Kat replied, and walked away. Once she had, Grandma reached up, pressed her hands against the side of my face, and said, "What was once has come again. You will be fine." Then she left me standing there. I thought about that for a few minutes and couldn't make heads or tails of it. The best I could think of, it was some damn *Dine* cryptic goodbye shit.

Ty drove us out of there, and we proceeded to bump and thump our way to where ever the hell we were going. We rode in silence for the first twenty minutes or so. Ty broke it by asking me, "You don't mind if I ask you some questions about...you know...some of the stuff I heard that you did?"

"No. Go ahead."

I stretched my bad leg out and shifted in the seat. Kat whispered in my ear," You're going to need that bandage changed soon." I just grunted in reply and waited for Ty to spit it out. "I mean, you have been around since the beginning. I read every graphic novel about you I could. I still see them sometimes, but the paper quality is pretty bad. You don't look like how you look in those, you know."

"No shit?" I had seen some of the graphic novels way back when. I thought they were funny for about ten minutes, and then I got pissed. They made people I had cared about into jokes. None of the sweat, pain, and stink of death that had been a constant backdrop to life in the first years was mentioned. Plus, I came off looking pretty damn good, which instead of flattering I found irritating. I didn't know there were still paper versions circulating.

"I know they were exaggerated and all that, but even if it was half true it was..." He paused, I saw his teeth flash as he grinned, "I know, it sounds stupid, but it was inspiring."

Kat snapped at him, "Bullshit, Ty. I've heard the stories, and it was a tragedy. Everything that comes after was, too."

I was beginning to feel like I was invisible. Ty ignored her and continued, "You knew Max! The man that runs the North. And you were friends with Ninja! He leads Sword and Raven Legion. They haven't been beaten since the Battle of Ohio! Is it really true the old gods fight with them? Even the *Lakota* ride with them now."

"It wasn't the Battle of Ohio." I said flatly. "It was the Fucking Massacre in Ohio."

Kat hissed something in *Dine* at him. My guess it was, "Shut up!" It was good advice, if it was because I really didn't want to talk about the good old days. Kat and Ty rode in tense silence for a bit. I just rode. I wasn't feeling all that well. I was cold. Colder inside than I should be. The antibiotics weren't doing their job, or something else was going on inside me that shouldn't be. I buried it. I needed to focus.

"Tell me about who we are seeing and why."

I thought Ty would answer, but instead it was Kat who did. Either he was still smarting from whatever she had hissed at him, or Kat had the better conections. Or, maybe she just liked taking charge, which wouldn't come as a surprise to me. "We are going to see the Navajo Mountain Chapter. Both Ty and I belong, and they, well, our Chapter is different. We didn't move off our lands when the Feds came to force every one off. We knew that, and this was over two hundred years ago, that it was our land, and we weren't going to leave. We..."

"Any chance this was because they couldn't find you?"

I had her. I smiled. She didn't laugh until Ty did. Then she muttered, "Well, maybe." Ty told me, "There will be people from other Chapters there. We don't make decisions based on what a couple of people tell us to do. We talk it over first."

"A lot of talking over," Kat added.

"So, what are they talking over?"

Ty got serious again and said, "Organizing to protect our nation and people."

I wanted to say, "A little late aren't you?" but I decided not to. It was pretty rare in my experience that any group or individual got their act together except at the last minute. Instead I went with, "What's a Chapter?" I already had a good idea. It sounded like something a white guy from the government would think up as a nice way of saying "tribal band". I bet the word "empowerment" was in there somewhere, too.

The two of them went on and on about tribal politics, who was going to be there, and who I should pay attention to. I didn't listen. Instead I ran through the street layout of Page, where I thought were the strong points, and how I would assault them. Of course, I didn't have any assault troops, and I wasn't up to doing any shoot-and-scoot, but it was better than listening to them. I was thinking about how I would approach the Bridge, and whether I would want to bypass the city when I heard Kat say, "You're not listening, Gardener." I ignored the undertone of scold. Funny how I never heard that until after I slept with them.

I told the both of them, "I was leading troops when you were dreaming about what it be like to get laid. I have sized up more minor functionaries, and shot them when needed, than there is people in your Chapter. I don't do politics, nor do I tolerate them being run on me. I'll listen, as long as they keep it short. Otherwise, I am going to sleep. Hopefully after eating something that has sugar in it." That shut them up.

About thirty minutes later we pulled into the parking lot of the Navajo Mountain Chapter house. It wasn't very big, and it looked like three pointy-roof small wood houses that had been nailed together to make one almost big house. I figured someone must have gotten a deal on small pointy-roof module houses back in the day.

The parking lot was the usual interesting mix of vehicles. Horses and horse-drawn carts. Bicycles that were all tucked up next to the building's walls so they wouldn't get run over. A couple of motorcycles and two ancient SUV's that probably ran on bio fuel. I had noticed that battery cars weren't big out here, except as carriages for the horses to pull. Mercedes Benz smart cars were the preferred model in most places, but I doubt if many were ever used out here before. This was truck land once, and their skeletons, or what was left of them after being stripped, were everywhere.

We did the, "How are ya's" and "Hey's" as we walked towards the entrance. Kat had told me somewhere in the journey getting here how important it was to "see" each person I met or looked at. I just grunted, and said "Got it." The problem with people, in my mind at least, was they always assumed someone new was an idiot when it came to their local pond. Ponds were ponds. A big fish, a couple of other almost big fish, usually wanting to be the big fish. Their school of followers, a couple of lurkers, and a few low level predators. The real predators, the ones that lived for blood, they never came to the pond meetings. Probably because they never got invited.

I also knew how to look at people and greet them. Spending a few years learning what passed for law enforcement covered that in detail. Greet everyone, check them out, give them a threat rating, and move on. Before I grasped that, I had thought it was just bullshit politicking to talk to everyone you came across, mostly because then you had to listen to them. Then, there was the quicker method. I thought of it as "brushing the buttons", just enough contact to generate a short response, not enough contact to actually generate a conversation, but you still got to take a quick snapshot of them.

The first thing I noticed when we walked into the building was the smell. The smell of a group of people packed in like this was another data point to be taken in. Did they stink wrong? If they did it wasn't a good sign. There was honest stink, poor hygiene stink, sick stink, and fear stink. This was wood fire and sweat, plus some bean emissions, an honest stink. A long time ago me and Ninja had been talking about how to read a crowd in a room, and had come up with fifty different variables that we read in the first couple of minutes.

Then there was the "flow", for lack of better words. When I was younger, I had thought of it as a mystic current that the world generated; that only those who had been gifted by a higher power could read. Now I was more inclined to believe it was a highly tuned survival sense that was constantly updated by experience. I walked down the aisle left for me, as people moved out of the way just enough to get in a better position to stare at me.

I shrugged off Ty and Kat's help in walking and ignored their whispered comments, which when summarized, said I was supposed to wait and get called up to the podium. I don't wait. It pisses some people off when I do that, but I can't say that I care. Of course, I wasn't doing my manly confident stroll, either. It was more of a lurch, which I knew didn't quite make the impression I was used to. That did bother me. A lot of what I did was built around getting an edge, and appearance was part of it. A bitter small voice whispered to me, *"You're a fucking cripple now. Give it up."* I ignored the voice, but it still stung. Not as much as what I saw in some of the eyes of people I passed. The pity rankled, while a few were amused. One of them, a young guy with his own hardware worn like mine, was appraising me, and I could tell he liked what he saw. I stopped when I saw that. I needed to, plus, it was time to make a point. I stared at him. I didn't smile. I just stared and watched him run through his card deck of reactions. That alone told me enough. People like me, when faced off, don't have any cards to run. We are ready to go all the time, anytime, anywhere. It's why we live. For me, it was all I had left. He folded. I moved on. It was another show time in another town.

# Chapter 8

The podium was on a platform which would require me to climb a couple of steps. I decided not to. Instead, I turned and looked at the crowd, sweeping them with the "measured stare" while waiting for silence. When I got it, I let it hang for a couple of seconds before I said what I had to say.

"Thank you for allowing me to stand here before you. You know who I am. You know what I have done. I understand what you want, and that is to preserve your way of life against what you believe is coming."

I paused here, and checked for people nodding in agreement and not off to sleep. That was something I was known to do once upon a time in meetings of any kind. No one here was. This usually was the point when I began telling them that it could be done. Over the years I had said it enough that I could recite it in my sleep. It was something like this: It would be hard and they would have to become harder people than their enemies to do it, but they were brave and they were motivated. All they needed was training, leadership, and to be pointed in the right direction.

I didn't tell them that. It stuck in my throat. Instead, I looked at them and smelled the burning houses, fields, and saw the bodies that would come next. They weren't the right people, and to become the right people would destroy them as a nation. I didn't have a problem with that, as much as I was also tired of what would be needed. I had left the north over it, and I wasn't going to start now. Combat , especially personal, I lived for. Total war and annihilation of the enemy was none of that.

Instead, I told them, "I am not the right man for you. Sorry." I ignored the buzzing of the crowd, the shouted questions, the muttered nasty comment or two. Instead, I made my way to Kat and Ty and said, "Get me out of here." We had almost made it to the door when I heard someone say loudly, "We don't need him. We can do this ourselves." I stopped dead and slowly turned around to face him and the people who, for the most part, didn't seem too upset to see me go.

"You want to know why I said I can't help you?"

I paused and waited for the nods, the muttered or shouted "Yeahs!" When I got them, I continued with, "Because I'm not sure you know what you ask. Not only for yourselves, but as a people. They will come. They always do. They will be well armed, used to killing, raping, and taking. They will always have the edge until the end, when you, you as a people, have your backs to the wall, and you're seeing all you lived for just days, or usually minutes, away from extinction. You thought the white man was bad? You have seen nothing yet. There will be no reservations for the losers or mercy this time. There is no mercy anymore. No one can afford it now. There is just survival. That is where their edge is. They know, I mean *know*, in a way you can't imagine, that they have to find a place to live or they will die. Oh, yes, they will come."

They were silent now. Their shadows, thrown from the lanterns that provided the light, were elongated, still, and listening. I was talking to them but seeing other places, other times, and the gnawed bones of children and adults who believed in the lies whispered by fools who deluded themselves to their final moments on earth that mercy was hard wired in everyone.

"Before you ask what can be done, I want you to ask yourself this first; can I kill? I don't mean in battle with honor

60

and against an opponent armed as you are. You will have to slaughter them in battle and the wounded afterward. No mercy. You will need to find their camps and kill every male that can walk. Their women, all but the young or useful, must die. You will have to do this until they stop coming, because there is none left alive to come. I can't help you because I can't do that. I won't do that." I turned away and walked out the door.

I was glad to get back in the truck, and even happier when we got rolling. The whole meeting thing had left a sour taste in my mouth, my head hurt, and I thought I could smell my leg rotting. My boots were pinching, and I wanted my old ones back. Plus, Kat wouldn't look at me and Ty had changed. "*Fuck,*" I thought. "*Fuck. Fuck. Fuck.*" I added a, "*Tough shit,*" too, but I wasn't sure if it was for them, me, or both. I also really didn't care...almost.

"So, where we going, Gardener?"

Ty's question caught me by surprise. I didn't know. I thought about my options. Back to the room, if I still had it. More than likely it was being watched, which meant was I up to shooting more Apaches, Feds, or fools? Yeah. I was okay with that, but I had a better idea. Perhaps I could squeeze another night out at Grandma's hogan, hopefully get a little loving from Kat, and sleep a lot better. I was more okay with that. So I told him, "How about bunking with Grandma for another night? Maybe you can give me a lift into town tomorrow, and I can mosey around and see if there is anymore Apaches that need killing." I liked saying "mosey", and ever since I had come west I had tried to use it whenever I could.

"It's '*Inde*', Gardener. Not Apache," Kat told me.

"Whatever."

"And, yes, I think we can spend another night at Grandmother's. You do plan on leaving her something … don't you?" The iron in her voice banged on my nerves. I looked over at her face, profiled by the light of the moon. It wasn't radiating lust for me. I didn't bother to answer. About thirty minutes later, in a more subdued voice, she asked, "Will it really be that bad?" I almost lied. Instead, I told her the truth, "Yeah. It always is. It always is."

It was about ten minutes later when we saw the fire.

"Hey. That's a fire!" This was Ty's contribution. He cut off Kat, who was telling me no one said 'mosey' anymore, including her grandfather. "Stop the truck." I said this calmly, which meant Ty didn't listen, or if he heard me, he wasn't listening fast enough. I tried again. "STOP the Fucking TRUCK!" That worked. I caught Kat across the chest with one arm trying to stop her from eating the dashboard, while I braced myself with my other hand. The truck may have come with seat belts, but they had long ago broken or been cut away except for the driver's side.

Kat yelled, "God damn!"

"Shut up. Ty listen to me. Kill the lights, put us in reverse, and then slowly move us backward about a quarter mile to the turn off we passed. Pull into it and keep your foot off the brake pedal."

I said this calmly and quietly, and it got through to Ty. He was an EMT. He knew emergencies and how to react. I knew he would key in to the calmness in my voice after yelling and figure out we had a problem. He did, and I was glad. My Plan B was putting a gun to his head. That would have been awkward.

Kat asked, "What's going on, Gardener?" I had seen movement silhouetted by the flames. I was also pretty sure I had seen horses off to one side. My leg may be hurting, and my boots were too fucking tight, but I could still see and hear better than almost anyone within seven hundred miles.

"It's a raiding party."

"Who?" Ty asked.

"I have no idea. From the look of those flames they

should be about done.  If they move this way, I want to be ready for them."

I was mentally inventorying what we had against what they might have.  Horses made it more complicated but still doable.  If the odds were too high against us, then we would let them go by and see if Grandma was still alive, which I doubted.

The desert at night when the moon is out is a place of shadows as much as it is of light.  Night in the desert is when the predators awaken and slough off the heat of the day, and feed their hunger pains.  Some people never get comfortable moving at night in the land of night shadows, be it forest or sand.  I wasn't born to it, but I took to it and made it my own.  I was confident that alone gave me an edge which was considerable.

We made it to the turnoff and Ty slowly backed us down the road.  Road was a word that meant one thing to people of my generation and another to Kat's.  I remembered when the word "road" meant well maintained two- and four-lanes of asphalt, where you could drive at eighty miles per hour and watch terrain that might as well be the moon pass by outside of your air-conditioned bubble.  Kat had never seen that and probably never would. Her mental picture of a "road" was closer to what we had just left.  Something that had a black tar foundation in some places.  A surface that was made of a long-lost material the ancients had created.  Over it were drifts of sand, washouts roughly patched, and places where the only reminder that a road had even been there were signs for speed limits, and places that only existed in the minds of those of us who still remembered what once was.

I told them, "Find somewhere in the next few minutes to hide it, at least break the silhouette, if you get hung up -- leave it.  Take Kat, and move at least one hundred yards from the vehicle once you stop."

"Where are you going?"

I grabbed her by the back of the head and pulled her face to me. It took a couple beats for her lips to soften. Too bad that was all the time I had. I popped the door open and fell out. It wasn't pretty, even as slow as Ty was going, exiting a moving vehicle is always awkward at best. No spasm of pain from my body or the sound of gear or clothing ripping, and best of all I wasn't going to be picking gravel out of my palms. It was a winner as far as I was concerned.

## Chapter Nine

There was a sandstone ridge that ran fairly close to the hogan. The end of it, which was mostly submerged in sand, was the what I had climbed up to stare at the sky what seemed like a million years ago. I ran at a slow trot, whose lurching motion smoothed out enough after a bit that I actually felt semi-normal. My guess was that I was stretching what ever muscle needed it out. I could hear them clearly now. They were speaking a mix of what had to be Apache, English, and I thought I heard some Mexican slang. They talked too much, that was for sure. The horses were quieter but I could smell them, hear them stomp their feet, and the raspy sound of tails twitching. They weren't happy about the fire.

I dropped and crawled the final ten feet, until I got to a place I could observe them from. It was a man-sized chunk of sandstone that had broken off from the rest of the family and run off on its own. It hadn't gotten far.

They were wrapping it up. One of them had just finished scalping Grandmother, and was laughing as he shook his pelt at a couple of his buddies. Grandmother wasn't dead yet but headed there fast. Her face was a mess. Scalping does a number on the facial muscles, and she was looking like a stroke victim who had a total face meltdown. Her fancy cloth layer of dresses and been pushed up past her thighs at one point but she had managed to pull them down far enough to cover herself. I never understood why some men felt the need to rape old women, but I had killed a few of them before for it. I had been told scalping was the new thing to do down this way. They were right, it looked like.

It was time to show them what I thought about it. I pulled the Winchester 30-30 from Sword's scabbard on my back. There were eight of them. Three were already on horseback, one of them was holding Scalper Boy's horse's reins, two were staring at their collection of loot that was spread out in front of them on a blanket, one was pissing on the burning hogan and shouting something about his fire hose to the guy who had been stuck tending the horses.

They were armed with the usual mix of aging rifles, handguns, large knives, and what had to be a lance. That was a first for me. I liked that. I collected firsts these days, and it been a while since the last one. I used iron sights because that was what I had learned on, and because I didn't like scopes. My feeling was if I wasn't close enough to hit you without a scope, then I had screwed up. Plus, and people seemed to think this was strange considering it was coming from me, but I thought drilling someone from four hundred feet out or more was impressive, but wrong on a level I could never get past.

I got up on one knee, ran my target list through my head one more time, and shot Scalper Boy in the sternum. I was aiming for his Adam's apple, but he moved and I never really was as good with a rifle as I was with my revolvers. I levered another round and shot the horse that was waiting for the departed Scalper Boy dead center in the side. It screamed, I said a silent, "Sorry," swung to my right, and nailed the guy who was bringing up the rest of the horses.

My original plan was to spook the horses, kill the ground guys, and then deal with the riders who would, hopefully, still be trying to get their mounts under control. It was cold, efficient, and maximized mine and anyone with me odds of survival. It had been a while, decades, since I had screamed her name and charged a battle line, house, or band of warriors. I had replaced it with cunning and the cold steel desire to kill as many Feds, or whoever, as I could, and live to do it again.

This time was different. In between shooting one of the guys who were staring at the blanket and counting his loot, the mounted ones began shooting back at me, along with the the man who thought he had a fire hose. Not accurately, but that would change soon.

That's when a wind as cold as ice blew through me. It was good. It was more than good. It was like being touched by lightening, god, and the woman you loved all at once. It had been a while, a long while, but I knew the feeling and welcomed it back like I would an old friend, if I had any.

I stood up and screamed her name, that cold-hearted bitch whose name hadn't passed my lips in years. "Freya!" Then I started walking down the hill shooting horses. I wanted them on foot. I wanted them to come to me. I wanted to see their faces when I killed them, and most of all I wanted them to see mine.

What happened next, as usual, didn't flow like a movie. It was time compressed into fragments. Snapshots of images, smells, and sound. Random thoughts like advertisements from another planet flashed in my brain. Lightening strikes of words, twisted into thought, and just as quickly gone. My world, when I enter this zone becomes layers, and I respond without thinking, fear, or pain. All I feel is joy, and it feels so good. So very good.

A horse, its neck arched, snorting and eyes rolling, drops slowly on its forelegs to the ground. My rifle is empty. I reach back, drop it in its sheath, and draw both my Rugers. I feel fluid, my leg is working for now, I am me again. The me that once was.

A round smacks me in the chest. A handgun, from the feel. I think, "Body armor for the win!" It's Hoser. He isn't bad, but I'm better. He dies. Running at me full speed is a face screaming in rage. He is wearing war paint. How unoriginal. He dies, too. I keep moving. I'm going downhill now. Fast. I feel like I am flying. One of the formerly mounted guys is standing behind a down horse. I keep coming. I don't pull the triggers. His nerve breaks. He fires but misses. I jump onto the horse and launch myself at him. Something, gear? The horse? My leg? Whatever it was, the angle isn't what I had ran in my head, but I don't care. I hit the ground off balance and stumble. It doesn't matter, and he knows it. I see it in his eyes just before I make impact. He knows who I am. I am death, and I won't stop coming.

He is down. I smell his stink, see his eyes widen, and then I begin beating his face to a pulp with one Ruger while keeping the other ready. I don't have any more time for this. I jam the barrel in his eye, pull the trigger, and roll off of him.

Only one of them is left, and I want him.  No one escapes.  I hear, "No mercy," in a voice from a world gone, and I scream my rage at what was taken.  I keep rolling.  No reason why, I just do, and it was the right thing to do.  The sand I had just rolled out of, and the guy who I just provided an eye-opener twitched with the multiple rounds of a machine pistol running full tilt.  Somebody had just spent a month's pay, at least.

The timing was unfortunate for me.  Both Rugers were empty.  I still had the Navy Colt, but I noticed the lance I had seen earlier was laying on the ground less than a foot away, and I grabbed it.  The burst had died off far too soon, a jam, and I heard him say something that probably translated to, "Motherfucker!"

I stood up.  He was about twenty paces away.  I grinned at him.  He didn't grin back.   I hurled the lance at him.  Much to my amazement, and from the look on his face, his, it punches solidly into his chest. I watched as he reached out, wrapped his hands around it, trying to pull it out, and drops to his knees. I shot him in the head with the Colt anyway. Fuck 'em. Always better to make sure they're dead then to assume it.

I look around. A chunk of of the hogan falls off  and lies burning in the sand. Most of the structure is gone. I hear at least two horses crying. I begin reloading while I move backward out of the firelight. Never assume its over and never stand in the spotlight. I'll move again as soon as I reload, wait a few in another spot, and then begin walking the perimeter slowly. Just to make sure. Then I'll have to kill the injured horses. I'm not looking forward to it.

## Chapter Ten

"Oh, my God!" was the first thing out of Kat's mouth, quickly followed by, "Grandmother!" Her and Ty went running to where Grandmother was lying in the sand. For a second I considered going to her side, but I decided instead to go find a rock to sit on while the drama ran down. It didn't last long, and I didn't expect it to. She was pretty hardcore, and Ty was an EMT, or what passed for one around here, and they had grown up in a tough world. I figured I had about five minutes of star gazing at most before they were done. I was wrong. It took her all of two minutes. Helped by the fact that Grandmother was dead, I'm sure. I had found that Kat's generation were realists about death, blood, and other facts of life that were once considered "gross" by the people of mine.

I heard, "Where the hell is Gardener?" from Kat, and I decided to get up off my ass and mosey on over. Ty replied, "Damn. I think he killed every one of them. This is fucking amazing." They didn't hear me walk up behind them, so I startled the hell out of them when I said, "No. Just doing what was needed." I wanted to say, "I'm just a simple cowpoke," but this wasn't the right audience, if one even existed. They both stared at me like I had just dropped in from another planet. I told Kat, "We can bury her here if that is okay with you."

"Sure. That's fine."

Then Kat added, "I'm glad you killed them, Gardener."

"Yep."

I told Ty, "I want you to shoot the horses. I'm going to see if we got any live ones, and see what I can find on them."

"Shouldn't I look for live ones?" was Ty's reply.     "No. You'll try and heal them. I just want them to talk to me."

First, I went and retrieved the lance, and it was a bitch to get out. Definitely a one-shot weapon. I ended up having to roll him over on his stomach and slide him down the length of the shaft to get it loose. It had a wicked piece of steel on the end that looked freshly forged. All the cool feathers fell off, though, in doing that, or ended up lodged in his lungs or somewhere. I had to wipe the shaft off with his shirt, and it was going to require further cleaning later. Then again, it might be a decent stain, kind of redwood-looking and all. I was laughing to myself over that when Ty yelled out, "Got a live one here, Gardener!"

"How live is that?"

Ty looked at me, puzzled, so I added, "Does he got another thirty minutes or more left?"

He looked down at the survivor, who all I could see of was a leg. My guess was he got pinned when his horse went down. "Oh, yeah. At least.

"Make sure he doesn't have a weapon, then finish the horses, and take care of Grandmother. I'll be over in a few."

I worked real hard at keeping my voice level and the irritation out of it. "*Fucking rookies,*" is what I thought. It had been a while since I had worked with people who were this clueless about the basics.

I started checking bodies to make sure they were dead, using the same method I had used since the beginning. The lance made it easier. I leaned on it and then kicked them in the head. I left the pat down and weapons collection for later. I wanted to make sure I talked to the survivor. No one else was alive. I would have been pissed if they had been.

Ty and Kat were hovering over Grandmother. They couldn't figure out how they were going to dig a hole. Yeah. Rookies. I could hear them arguing over who was going to walk back to the truck to get the shovel as I walked over to say hello to my new friend. I sat down on the haunch of the horse that had him pinned. Their horses weren't all that big, which was fine because none of these guys had been very big, either. They were all post- PowerDown born, except for two of them. The young ones coming up were kind of on the scrawny side compared to the males who were grown, or were close to it, when the economy tanked. This was one of the older ones. I was glad. They cracked easier then the young ones, I had found. "How ya doing there?" I asked him.

"How's it look, asshole? I got a dead horse on my leg."

"Bet that hurts."

He was doing a pretty good job of eating the pain but it hurt, I could see it in his eyes.

"Yeah. Want to get it off me?"

"No. Not really."

His eyes narrowed. "So, you're really Gardener."

"Yep."

"You'll be dead soon."

I laughed. "Right. Well, you'll be dead sooner."

"I'm not afraid of dying."

He sounded like he meant it, too. "That's nice." I told him. Then I reversed the lance and drove the head into his stomach and pulled it back out. He yelped, just a small little yelp, then groaned and grabbed at his gut. Blood was already starting to darken his shirt.

"I'm not going to kill you right away. I'll just leave you out here for the buzzards and maybe the coyotes. You have wild dog packs around here? Yes, I believe you do." He called me a mean name. I laughed. "So...want to hear my deal?" He didn't respond. Well, he snarled, but technically I didn't consider that a proper response. "Okay. You talk to me and I put one in your head if I'm satisfied. If not? I leave you." Much to my delight, a coyote pack started singing. His unease over hearing this was palatable. "You're really an asshole, Gardener," he told me through gritted teeth.

"Yeah. So I've been told."

I waited and watched, waiting for him to begin to really feel the pain and let the reality soak in like the blood into his shirt.

"So, you have a name?" I asked him after a few minutes.

"No."

"Hmmm...How do you get your mail"?

He looked at me blankly for a second, barked a one syllable laugh, and said, "That world's gone, Gardener. Long gone."

He and I looked at each other, and what passed between us was what I called "The Knowledge." Every once in a while you would be talking, sometimes in a group, sometimes not, usually there would only be two of us old enough to understand, and somebody would say something about the old world. You and the other survivor from then would lock eyes for a second and exchange the look. That look said, *"We know. We were there. The rest of you don't. It's just tales from a world you can't even comprehend, but we do. We were there."* Usually it was followed by a flicker of sadness, of pain, of old memories that still retained their sharp edge, and then it was locked away. A ripple that passed unnoticed unless you had "The Knowledge."

"Yeah. Now that we had our moment," I told him, "let's talk about today. What the fuck were you doing here?"

"Looking for you."

I checked his shirt out, perhaps I had gone a little too deep prodding him. Time to skip over superfluous stuff.

"Any more of you?"

"Yeah. We ain't alone, either. Some weird shit is going on here. Should have stayed home this time."

He paused, sighed a low, "Oh, man," and shut his eyes for a couple of beats.

"Hey. How many?"

He opened his eyes. I could see he was slipping away, shock was already there, and death was slipping through the door into his room.

"Go in peace, no name."

He blinked and was gone. I watched his skin color change as his life slipped away and wondered why the hell I had said that.

I didn't think about it very long, maybe all of one beat before I switched my brain over to processing important stuff like the fact I was hungry, my feet hurt, and now I was going to have to come up with a new plan or two or three. I didn't bother moving off of my horse haunch chair. Instead, I did a quick scan of the scene and focused on how Kat and Ty were doing.

He was digging. She was staring at the hole he was creating. An efficient allocation of labor. Not. Once upon a time I would have got up and suggested she find something to do, or her squad leader would have. I let it go. I liked her. A lot. I had rediscovered sex with her, and found I liked that a lot, too. So I sat and ran what what No Name had told me, and what I thought it meant.

Killing me was no big deal. There were more of them which wasn't a big deal, either. What it did mean was whoever was in charge was somewhere else, probably in town or camped near it. It also told me they had enough people that this leader could send eight people out and still have enough left to maintain security. He, or less likely but still possible she, would have come in person with them unless there was enough people left behind or something was going on that they didn't feel comfortable leaving. That meant more than ten, but less than twenty as the grazing and hunting around here wasn't good enough for more then that. Even then, they would have to move every couple of days.

Or, was it the feds? This was a long way for them to reach out, and they were having problems elsewhere. The people they had in town had been for a negotiation and business venture, not a strike team, or they wouldn't have had to hire contractors for security. They might send in a team to kill me, god knows they hated my guts enough, but I didn't plan on sticking around long. Their advantage was the same as it had always been, tech, but I was willing to gamble that they wouldn't send any of their remaining drones for a couple of days.

That gave me a window of forty eight hours to wrap it up here and begin my advance back to Salt Lake. Once I got us into Saint territory the drone-masters would be less willing to follow due to political reasons. It also helped that the Saints had their own anti-drone tech and didn't hesitate to use it. Like everything else the feds created, drones weren't cheap but countermeasures were. Directed EMP blasts were easy to do and if you weren't using electronics. The advantage was all yours. I figured that was a large enough window of time that I could get my old boots back, eat, get laid, and kill some more people.

When I saw them moving Grandmother into the grave, I got off my ass and walked over to be a part of the ceremony. It was brief. Ty spoke, but since he didn't use English I had no clue what he said, but I could guess as I had been to enough funerals. Kat said her piece and started crying at the end. I put my arm around her waist and instead of pulling away she leaned into me, which was nice. I was glad I had the Lance to use as a third leg, though.

Whatever had happened that made me able to move like I used to had slipped away. I hoped it would come back, but I wasn't going to count on it. They both looked at me after they had spoken, so I mentioned to god she was a good cook, and although I hadn't known her long she was a decent person with a good heart. That went over well. We were done, or we were just starting if you looked over your shoulder at the dead bodies behind us.

## Chapter Eleven

"Now what, Gardener?" Ty asked me.

"Plenty of horse meat. You think you could get some people here before it starts going bad?"

He pursed his lips and looked up, I guess for inspiration, and said, "Yeah, for some of it. By the time word gets out and people can get their transportation together, well, we might get a third of it at best. Need to gut them, too. That's going to draw critters." Kat spoke up, telling the both of us, "How's this for a plan? We cut off what we can and throw it in back of the truck. I can sell it in town. We drop Ty at the Chapter House, they can send runners, and we meet back here." Ty looked at me, I shrugged and told them, "Sure, why not. I can pick up my boots and see if I can find out anything more about what is going on." Ty thought about and asked me, "Won't that be dangerous. I mean..." He didn't finish the sentence. Kat was laughing and I was almost smiling. "Yeah. Right. Damn, this going to be messy." He was right. It was.

We had to give up on cutting up the horse meat after a while. There wasn't enough light to work by, and we were all tired. Working with sharp knives by moonlight when you're tired was a great way to end up hurt bad. Nowadays my guess was infections killed more people than guns did, which was saying something. Child birth was back to being a big deal, and so was breaking a bone. Since PowerDown Women's rights had taken a major step back, at least a hundred years worth of stepping. Not because men decided it. Childbirth, kid shepherding, and the division of physical labor made it happen. The attitudes that went with it a hundred years ago had tried to make a comeback, but with women who knew how to use a gun, and probably had, it didn't get far. I had noticed most of the old-school fundie communities disarmed their women.

Then again there were women like Kat, who hadn't stepped back and never would. She would, and probably had, paid for that attitude. The *Dine* culture, from the little I knew, was unusual in that women had always had a voice in how things were run. It occurred to me this might be why they were never a warrior society, and I almost asked Ty what he thought but decided not to. It might start a conversation, and I wasn't really in the mood.

I halfway listened to Ty and Kat talk about what restaurant would be best to sell the meat at. There were only two, so you would think that would have been a conversation that only lasted two minutes, but no. Then it was who would have a truck or a cart near enough to help harvest the rest. They they talked about what to do with the Apache bodies. I went to sleep, only waking up every couple of minutes when my head bounced up and down harder than normal as we hit another hole, stone, or washout in the road.

I sleepwalked through the off-loading of the meat, and when the palaver began about what had happened and what needed to happen, I told Kat I would be in the truck waiting. Since we weren't moving, I actually drifted off into a deep sleep. Something that was unusual for me, as I very rarely did unless I felt I was in a secure place to do it.

I had been having nightmares since I was old enough to remember. The only difference over the years was the theme and my reactions inside the dream. One of the reasons I slept alone for the last few decades was my habit of punching and kicking whoever was lying next to me. Not intentionally, it was a reaction to the battles I was fighting in the dreamworld. I always felt bad about it, apologized profusely, and after the third time it happened I was back to sleeping alone. I never knew when a dream was going to be a nightmare. They just were.

This one started nicely enough for a nightmare. I was sitting in the woods, on a log screened by some half-assed bushes from the meadow that was on the other side. The day was sunny, and in this dream I felt young, which was one of the few good things I liked about dreams. Then it went downhill rapidly. The sunlight faded. In my dream, I looked up at the sky to see if clouds were rolling in, but there was no sky. I looked back down. The bushes were gone, and a crow, a large one, a very large one, as in the size pf a pony, was there instead.

I said, "Hello, crow."

"Hello, Gardener."

I recognized the voice and told myself, "Screw this, I'm going to wake up." In the dream I was blinking my eyes rapidly, but the damn crow was still there.

"I'm still here." Then she giggled.

"Yeah. I noticed. Why the crow suit?"

"I don't know. I thought I would wing it?"

"That was lame, Freya. Lame as you showing up here."

The crow sighed, which I thought was kind of cool for some bizarre dream-reason.

"I thought we should talk."

"Why? I'm done with you. We went through all this a long time ago."

I was talking to nothing before I finished saying this, the crow disappeared and then Freya, the version I remembered, was standing there. Except ,she looked more like Cate

78

Blanchett than usual. I was okay with that. I liked Cate Blanchett a lot better. Then she ruined it by talking.

"What happened was just that. You never did understand what I showed you so long ago. I forgive you for that, and I have decided..."

"Forgive me?! FORGIVE ME?! Fuck you, bitch!" I was on my feet and running at her. I was going to beat the hell out of her. Then, maybe I would kill her, or die trying.

I woke up due to a combination of things, the foremost being pain and the other voices, one of which I recognized. The pain was from beating the hell out of the dashboard. My left hand hurt, and I was going to be seriously pissed if I had broken anything in it. The voice was Ty's, who was telling someone, "Hell, no. I'm not waking him up. You do it." I snapped my head around to see him and Kat staring at me from six paces away. Ty looked ready to run, and Kat actually looked concerned. I took a deep breath, looked up, blew it out, and told them, "I'm fine. Just a bad dream."

"No shit, man," Ty said.

"Yeah, no shit," I told him tiredly. "We ready to go?"

Kat answered for him, "Yeah, Gardener. We're ready. Give me the key, Ty."

We pulled out. I looked back to see who else was watching, and saw no one. Ty had gone back inside.

"You okay?"

"Yeah, Kat. I'm fine."

"I get bad nightmares, too. Lots of the older people do, too."

I grinned. I knew I was included in the "older people", but I didn't say anything. She didn't correct it, or tell me I wasn't one of the "older people", either. She watched me for a minute or two out of the corner of her eye, and realized I didn't have anything more to say on the subject, so she dropped it.

That made her smarter then 95% of the population I routinely dealt with.

We rolled on a bit and I watched as the false dawn put a little more light on the landscape. "Beautiful country," I said out of nowhere, and then mentally kicked myself. I hated people who made inane remarks just to fill airspace, and what I just said sure as hell qualified as one. She just smiled, reached over and rested her hand on my thigh, and said, "That was really impressive, what you did back there."

"Carve up horse meat?"

She looked at me like I was nuts. "No. Not that." Then she reached a little higher up on my thigh and squeezed.

"Oh, yeah. That."

She was smiling, the truck was slowing down, her hand didn't move as she touched the brake and shifted into park. She turned a little bit in the seat so she could look at me directly. The smile deepened, and she told me, "I want your baby." I didn't argue.

## Chapter Twelve

We were about three miles out of town when I told her to stop the truck as I wanted to walk into town.

"Okay, babe," was her reply. She hadn't stopped smiling, and that was a little weird hearing myself called ,"Babe." I wasn't sure if I liked it or not. I did like that smile. I was sure it was at least partly bogus, but I felt more studly than I had in a long time. I told her,"See you in town." She replied, "You got it." With that, a little wave of the hand, and a foot on the accelerator, she was gone. Damn, that muffler was shot. I stood there watching her pull away, and as I did, I found she had also driven off with my studly feeling. Left in its place was a little bit of foolishness, and a lot of alone. I shrugged it off and started walking. Not many minutes later I was cursing my loaner boots.

The air smelled clean and there was little to no wildlife noise. Not like Virginia, where every morning in good weather the birds, and an occasional paranoid squirrel, would be busy wildlifeing. Not here. Here is was snake slither and reptile crawl, except for the occasional jack rabbit making a run for it. I liked it most of the time. Having the Lance was turning out to be a big help. My leg was still acting up, but it was feeling a little better. My plan was to find a place to watch the town for a bit, go get my boots, get a shower, and change clothes.

Maybe even a shave. If I got real lucky, the place to eat might even have desserts.

Instead, I heard the sound of gunfire. A lot of it, and not handguns, either.

"*Damn. So, the Apaches finally asked someone for directions,*" was the first thing that went through my mind when I heard the noise start up. I started following the sound and ended up on the edge of the plateau or mesa, I was always getting those two confused, that the city of Page was built on.

Off in the not-so-far-away distance, the Apaches were trying to force the bridgehead on this side of the river and succeeding. On my right, a convoy of vehicles, horses, and a fair amount of people on bicycles was racing down, or close to the road from Page, to hit them from behind. They had balls, but they didn't have the .50 calibers mounted on trucks that the Apaches did. The convoy proceeded to get eaten alive. They did manage to accomplish one thing, and that was to distract the Apaches at the bridge, who started getting chewed up by the Navajo heavy weapons from their positions in the Beehive. What was really amazing, and something I hadn't seen in years, was the attacking Apaches had their families with them. I started scanning the desert and spotted even more of them hanging behind, waiting for the signal to cross or move into town.

I found a place to observe and got comfortable. I watched for about fifteen minutes and realized I was hot, hungry, and could be smelled from about a mile away from the horse blood. Plus, the flies were annoying the hell out of me. I decided to hell with it. It was time to go get my boots back while I could. The situation here was none too stable. It was time to get moving away from here. I would find Kat and ask her if she wanted to come with me, round up some transportation, and start us moving down some back roads.

I approached the town warily. As best as I could tell, not much was happening in town this early in the morning, which was a little hard for me to believe. I could smell wood smoke, horse shit, and horses. It's amazing how far off you can smell horses, and bread cooking somewhere. That made my mouth water and my tummy rumble.

The other thing that was bothering me was all the crows. What the hell was going on? A fucking crow convention? Plus, they were keeping their beaks shut. Crows like to talk, scold, and generally shoot the crow crap with each other. These were just hanging out, staring at me, staring at each other, staring off into space. Freya showing up in my dreams and all these crows was not what I considered a good omen. That, and the feel of the place had changed. Something wasn't right. The closer I got to the town, the stronger the feeling. It was the same feeling you get right before a storm, or just before you made contact with people who didn't like you and planned on showing it by shooting holes in you.

I was happy that the shoe repair place wasn't too far from the edge of the desert. Then again, nothing in town was. Once I got into town, I couldn't walk in a straight line because of having to weave around piles of horseshit, which was unusual. Piles never stayed in the street very long. Not because there was a community employed horse shit janitor. No, it was a valuable commodity because the sand here was not ideal for growing anything you really wanted to eat other then stunted corn. These were fresh ones, too.

I was already walking next to building walls and watching windows, so now I started easing around corners. I did slide past a window and caught a glimpse of a young lady getting dressed. That was both cheesy and cool. Mostly cheesy. Nice rack, though.

I eased around the last corner before the cobbler's, and saw the old man with the eye patch sitting in a folding chair out front watching me. He yelled out, "Whatcha doing, fella! Stealing chickens, or looking for boobies!" It took me a few beats to process "boobies" and put it in context. I felt my face flush, and it didn't help that he started cackling like a demented idiot, which I was sure he wasn't, but one step or two removed from. I kept walking, and when I was close enough that I didn't have to yell, I told him, "Shut the fuck up, old man." He just cackled some more. I brushed past him, resisting the urge to wallop him upside the head with the barrel of a gun. He told me, "She's waiting for you. You give her something sweet, and she might fix that bum leg of yours." I stopped dead, maybe a pace from the door, and quietly asked him, "You want to repeat that?"

"I said, talk sweet to her, and she might fix your leg. She used to be a nurse."

I knew that wasn't what he said, but I let it slide. Instead, as I turned the doorknob I said over my shoulder, "You got a scorpion on your shirt, by your armpit." His, "What?! What?! Where?!" making me laugh as I stepped to one side of the door to let my eyes adjust to the dimness.

She was waiting for me on the other side of the counter, just as old and tired looking as the last time. I stood there and stared at her; her eyes were brown, her breasts pendulous, and her smile stained. No, this wasn't Freya. This was just a woman stuck in a little town in the middle of nowhere, trying to make it through another day. A description that fit almost every woman I had met her age in the past few decades. She didn't bother with, "Hello." Instead she said, "The old man giving you a hard time?"

"No. You got my boots?"

"You got your ticket?"

"You never gave me a ticket."

She squinted at me for a couple of beats, and her face

changed. A raspy chuckle, a wheeze, and she said, "Oh, yeah. The magic boots man. My sister took care of that. Hold on." She shuffled off into the back, and I took a look out the window. The old man was gone, and the morning was giving way to afternoon. Nobody else was out in the street, and the town was quiet. Too quiet. I didn't like it. I turned around and she was there. Freya.

"Hey, Kid."

"Hey, Gardener."

"Who was the old lady?"

"My sister."

"Damn, she's ugly."

Freya laughed and sis's voice came from somewhere in the back, "I heard that."

"Yes. She didn't want believers, so she is stuck for now in her old shell."

"That has to suck."

Freya didn't laugh. Not even a smile. "It does." We stared at each other. I blinked first. She was the only person, and the person part was wrong, which didn't make it feel any better, who could do that to me. Her eyes, they led places I wasn't willing to go. For the first time, I wondered if Max looked away, too. I doubted it.

"I would love to kill you," I told her.

"I know."

I thought I detected a trace of sadness in her voice. I ignored it. "You deserve to die." She shrugged. "By your standards, I do. I wish I could tell you what I know, but instead I am going to help you learn it yourself."

I just stared at her. I really wanted to shoot her right between those pretty blue eyes, but I had tried that before. It didn't work then, and I doubted if it would now. Instead, I asked her, "How so, and whats the price?"

"Blood, and my name."

I thought about it.  Blood was not a problem.  Her name?  It was always about her, so that wasn't a surprise.  While I was mulling it over, she added, "I will take you back to what once was."  That jammed my thought processes up real quick.  I was also getting more suspicious by the second.  A quick ,"Night?" arc lit my brain up, but she wasn't that powerful.  So I told her, "Explain, Freya, and by the way, where the hell are my boots?"

She reached under the counter, came up with them, and dropped them on the counter with a thud.  As soon as her hand disappeared I had, without thinking, reached for my Ruger.  She smiled, gave a minute shake of her head, and said, "You really need to wash your socks more.  These were nasty."

"Right."

I grabbed them and sat down in one of the folding chairs used for customer seating.  Grunting, I began pulling off my loaners, telling her, "Take a whiff of these, they smell like honey and fresh mowed grass."  It was her turn to say, "Right."

She waited until I had pulled both boots on before telling me, "I will turn back the clock for you.  You will physically be the you that you were when we first met.  I will provide you video of the town, and I will return you what is rightfully yours.  You only have to solve a minor problem for me."

I thought about it while I admired my old boots.  I knew there had to be a catch, a nasty one, but I didn't really care.  I didn't like being a cripple, and most of the time I wasn't ready to die.  If I was going to, I wanted it to be in combat, not sitting in a room afraid to go outside.  I told her,  "You know, you could have shined them up a bit.  Most cobblers do."

"I'm not most cobblers, G.  What say you?  Time is running again."

"Hell, yeah.  Shower me with goodies and lets do this."

## Chapter Thirteen

She smiled at me, the woman was incredibly lovely when she did, and reached back under the counter. My hand had never moved off my gun, so we didn't have another little moment when she gently laid a burlap wrapped object on the counter where my boots had been. She looked at me calmly. I knew what it was, and my breath caught in my throat along with my heart. "Sword." I didn't say it as a question, either.

"Yes."

"I thought it was lost during the battle when..." I couldn't finish it. I couldn't.

"No, Gardener. Not lost. One of mine found it and brought it to me. You were thought to be dead, so I sent it back to my hall to wait for you."

"It never occurred to you to return it after I was found alive?"

She shrugged, "I got busy. Sorry."

I glared at her. Then I mentally shrugged it off. She was very good at acting like a flake when it suited her, but she was far from it. I unwrapped it, held it in my hand, and stared at her. I liked the flicker of uncertainty in her eyes. She had taken Sword back because it could hurt her, where nothing else would. It was of her time and named, although I could never pronounce it correctly, and I had gotten tired of her correcting me. She didn't speak to me for three days when I told I was going to call it Sword instead.

The blade was still blood smeared. It had never been cleaned since the last time I had used it. Memories of the day came flooding back in, none of them pleasant; the sound of automatic weapons burning ammo like they had an unlimited supply,which they did then, screams, dust in the air, noise of varying intensity from the explosions as they ripped us apart. We were falling back, trying to lose them, even the odds up by withdrawing deeper into the cover of the trees, but it wasn't working. I stopped the tape right there and refocused.

"Why, Freya? Why?" I genuinely wanted to know. She sighed, and for a second I saw the kid I knew once. "Because I was wrong about my power and theirs. They weren't warriors as I knew them. They were machines covered in metal and skin. They saw like I did, but so much better and farther. They had power then, G. Unimaginable power. The power of the gods in their prime, and they used it like angry children. I was so wrong then, but I learned. Oh yes, I did." She grinned, if you want to call it that. I responded to that grin and felt the killing madness touch me. I knew what she meant for I, too, had learned, and a part of me wished I hadn't. Their way was cold, methodical, and efficient. It was never my way, but I had used it to kill them. In doing so, it had quit being something I did and  became something I was.

I evicted the 30-30 from its sheath and returned Sword to its home. I shrugged my shoulders and pulled on one of the harnesses straps to balance it a little better. That done, I reached back, grabbed the hilt, screamed, "Freya!" and swept the blade forward and down into the counter. It was magic of the most special kind. Sword cleaved the wood like it was bone, and didn't stop until the end of the arc. Goddamn, if that didn't feel good. I pulled sword loose. That didn't go as smoothly, which was just as well because it gave me time to amp what I was feeling down a bit.

I got Sword free, stepped back, and much to my surprise I was panting a bit, not from exertion, rather the need to split some heads open and dump intestines on the ground. I wanted to hear screams of pain and smell their blood, fear, and urine as I sent them to hell. Freya had stepped back about four paces and was watching me warily.

I told her, "I'm good. Give me the background and I'm gone." She didn't seem convinced, but she told me what I had to do. It was pretty simple, at least the way she told it. I listened, did my own calculations, and realized no way in hell, even in my prime, was I going to make it through this alive, let alone unscathed. What I had was a hostage situation, inside an enemy held town. I was outnumbered significantly and the feds had a team on the way to kill me if the Apaches didn't.

The hostages were Navajo kids who were being held at the local school as backup plan. If the Apaches couldn't take the bridge one way, then lobbing a couple kids across to the other side with an ultimatum would. Also being held were their families, in a different part of the same building. With them, she mentioned, was a woman named "Kat." I really looked at her when casually mentioned that. Freya was always a jealous bitch, amongst a hundred other character flaws. I was going to say something, but decided not to. It wasn't worth it to me anymore. Oh, yeah, along the way there were scattered teams who were supposed to kill me before I got to the kids. If that didn't work, they would use the kids to flush me out and kill me for the reward and payback. She finished up with a smile and, "Any questions?"

"No. Give me a video feed and my legs back and I'm gone."

"G, you weren't listening to me, were you?"

"Yeah, I got the gist of it. There is many bad people who want to kill me and a hostage situation."

"G..." she sighed, "let me finish. You may be one of

the best single combat warriors I have ever known."

I raised an eyebrow.

"I go back a long way, Gardener..."

I let it slide. I knew I wasn't the best, anyway. Max was. I wanted to ask her if she knew Hector and Ajax, but I didn't want to end up discussing ancient history. Instead I said, "Okay."

"I brought you help, too."

I started looking around. It would be awkward and great to see Max again. Ninja, well, that would be truly outstanding. She was amused. "They're out back, G."

I left the 30-30, but I grabbed the Lance. Freya saw that and said, "You don't need it anymore, G." I stopped dead. She was right. I still felt great, and so did my leg. A wide smile split my face. I told her, "You're right. This is awesome! When the hell did that happen?" In a surprisingly gentle voice she told, "Enjoy it. The clock is ticking now. Follow me." When she turned her back, I did a little hop-skip-dance move, just for the pure joy of being able to. Damn, I hadn't realized how good it felt to have everything working, not hurting, and alive.

I followed her, damn, she had a great ass, and started looking forward to seeing Kat again. I bet we could find a closet somewhere. Oh, yeah! I focused again. Freya was talking again, something she loved to do. "Max and Ninja couldn't come. They're busy in Michigan and Ohio right now. We expect DC to fall within six months. Ninja asked for volunteers and your old unit, to a man, volunteered. He picked these from his personal security detachment." I knew they wouldn't come, but it still stung a bit. I was also curious about who and how many they had sent.

The backyard was not that big, but it had most of a privacy fence still intact. Freya motioned for me to go first though the back door, and I stepped out into the yard and to one side of the doorway. She didn't follow me. Instead she stood there, framed in the sunlight, and together we watched as four men quit drawing a map in the sand and stood up. They did it sharply, too. I watched them watch her. No doubt about it, they responded that quickly because they feared her, not cause she was wearing a long white cotton dress, and from the way the sun illuminated her, nothing else.

The next thing that struck me was how they were outfitted. My first thought was, "*Damn. They look more like the feds then the feds do.*" They were wearing khaki colored uniforms. Uniform meaning exactly that. They were all cut the same, which meant there was a factory making them somewhere. They all had helmets, fed style ones, once again all in the same color, their webbing and packs were made of leather, and they were extremely well armed.

Once again, all the equipment was standardized. AK-74's, the grenades looked like German WW II ones, but with a bigger can on the end. One man had a M240 machine gun, the belts for it looked different though, and a Barrett! These guys were packing some weight. I doubted they had, but if they walked here, they probably hated my guts. Two of them had sledge hammers on their backs in sheaths like I carried Sword. That told me they must have been doing a lot of city fighting before coming here. Once upon a time when I had been doing that we called sledges like that can openers, because we used them to knock holes in walls rather than use the doors.

I studied the men while she talked. It was a quick once-over because she didn't say much. What she told them was your basic, "Do right, die right, and make me and your families proud. I am with you." Then she left. I grinned when she did. A little Freya went a long way with me.

They were not what I expected, and I was glad. Everyone of the four in front of me, and what I could see of the two pulling security, were over thirty years old. Even more surprising was that two of them were officers, and the rest were senior NCO's. They all were wearing black stripes under their eye's, too. I had insisted on that way back when. No one was going to be wearing sunglasses around me. I was surprised it had stuck. They had also kept the Crow badge that was given for killing large numbers of the enemy under difficult conditions. What was different from what I remembered was, they were all heavily tattooed with intricate designs, including face tats, that probably meant something if you could read them.

They were staring back at me, most definitely taking my measure, too. Like the lady had said, "The clock was ticking," and I was beginning to feel uneasy. Fuck the speeches and idle chit chat about what was happening back in the NordLand. So I told them, "I want two fire teams of three. We move in bursts. First squad on me. Second squad burn this house down." I didn't bother to see if they understood or would burn the house down. Freya was gone, of that I was sure of. The rest of that motley bunch would vacate when they smelled smoke. People all over what had once been America hated my guts, and most of them did the hating from new places because I had burnt their town down. My rule had been if you helped the feds, you paid. Then you paid some more.

I hit the gap in the fence running while simultaneously mentally saying, "Freya, show me." Here was the test of how much she was willing to support me. One of her gifts was the ability to feed to the minds eye images of the area around you. She used birds, almost always crows, as her eyes, and at least in the beginning, you got raw data directly from the bird. It made for some fucked up video at times. Sometimes, if they were accepting direction, they would even look in windows or fly in and out of large buildings, like warehouses. It really wasn't all that different from a drone feed, except most drone operators were smarter, and had longer attention spans, than your run-of-the-mill, numb-nut crow.

Instead of Freya responding, I got the voice of a young woman with an Asian accent who told me, "This is Northern Arizona Control One, stand by for immediate area feed. *"Jesus, the fucking bitch is outsourcing?"* went through my head, but was quickly flushed by the imagery that followed. I stumbled and my vision blurred, the data flow was like a fire hose, "Goddamn it!" I yelled. "Simplify that shit now!" I heard a, "Standby," and got my vision and balance back. Just in fucking time, too.

An Indian male buttoning his fly stepped out of the side screen door of the house directly in front of me. He looked up at us, opened his mouth, and received the head of the Lance and six inches of the hardwood shaft chest center. He grabbed at the shaft, looked up at me in surprise, "*Damn, sticking people with lances is like back in the beginning when people always were looking surprised when I shot them,"* went through my head. I grabbed him by the handle, shoved him in front of me, and used him to power through the screen door ahead of me. He had switched from looking surprised to very unhappy about the time we went through that door, too. I was glad there wasn't any steps, as he didn't look like he was up to taking them.

I let go of the lance as we crossed the threshold and let him continue his journey into the next wall, while I drew both Rugers and changed course. The room I had just busted into was a kitchen, not a very large one, and it was occupied by an Indian woman who had just set down a cup and was reaching for the long-bladed knife laying on the tabletop next to a loaf of flat bread. I shot her, at the same time registering multiple thought fragments while I did. The thoughts ran together, they always did, "*Coffee???!! I smell! Bread. Good. Fuck. Both Dine?"* I kept going through the next doorway into a hallway.

I heard boots behind me. Both doors to the other rooms were open, the bathroom toilet need to be flushed, but since it was just piss they were probably waiting for a load to drop before they did. The bedroom was unoccupied, the bed looked freshly vacated. I yanked down the blanket covering the closet thinking, *"Why cover the closet but not the bathroom door?"* I got my answer. It had been made into a kid's room. It was empty, and felt like it had been for a while. I turned. One of my squad went pounding past me. I heard someone yell, "Clear!" I turned, and saw one of the two Captains was standing in the doorway looking at me. "We have a plan, sir?" I grinned at him and said, "I like the way you asked that, Captain. Yeah. Actually, I do. Head for the school. Free the hostages. Bug out." He didn't even blink. He just said, "Outstanding."

"Glad you liked it." I didn't grin. "Lets go."

I headed back the way I had come. As I went through the kitchen, I paused long enough to grab the woman's cup of coffee, drain it, and scoop up the bread. I ripped a piece off and threw the rest over my shoulder for the man behind me.

# Chapter Fourteen

My first inclination had been to charge through the middle of town by house-hopping until we got to the school. I felt good, real good. My body was running young, but my mind still had all the mileage of a hundred gunfights and small town raids, and it was telling me don't get everyone around you killed right away. Use your brain and your experience with the youth this time. Plus, I had the eye in the sky, and could work around the hot spots as much as possible.

Instead, I was going to head out of town. Page was built on a low mesa, and I wanted follow the edge around and come up to the school from behind. The town faded out fast on that side, and we would also have the advantage of being on the opposite of the mesa away from the bridge side action. From there we would have to cross a Catholic church grounds, a two-lane road, and then we could enter the school grounds by crossing a sandy field and some standalone classrooms that had been abandoned years ago.

We moved at a fast trot parallel to the cobbler's house for a minute before jumping down into a shallow wash that I knew would get deeper. Behind us, the house was beginning to burn nicely and smoke even nicer. Hopefully it would focus attention away from the direction I was headed. Now it was all going to be about moving fast and not stupid. Especially after we freed Kat and the kids.

I shouted in my head, *"Give me some video, Freya!"* I doubted if she would be the one who did. I had already found that out, but it was the only way I knew how to ask. My guess is they used special code words now, hell, somebody had probably worked "tactical" in there somewhere, I was sure. I added, "And don't fucking hose me!"

"Hello, Major Gardener." It was the same Asian accented voice, except now she sounded a lot like an awestruck sixteen year old girl. "This is Northern Arizona Control. My name is Keiku, and I will be your dedicated image controller. I understand you have not used..."

"Keiku."

"Yes sir?"

"Shut the fuck up and stay out of my head. Give me a quarter mile out, center on me, and run updates only on my command."

"Roger that. Conforming. Out."

She sounded a little miffed now. Too bad. I focused on the video. It was quiet. The only people moving in the area I was interested in was us, in two groups with fifty paces separating us.

"Keiku. Give me where we just left."

That wasn't quiet. They had a fast react team, and the way they were moving told me that it was a good one. I stepped up the pace. I couldn't hear anyone sucking wind, and I didn't expect to, either. Sweet Jesus, it was a joy to run like this. I let myself enjoy it for a few beats. Damn, when did this slip away? I knew, I mean really knew, that I was only cruising and there was still more like that waiting if I wanted it. Getting older, and the injuries had made so much of what I did something to be endured physically. This was nothing. It was fun again. I had forgotten how good it felt to move well and effortlessly, to feel like I was in my element instead of fighting it. I leaped a scrub bush instead of going around it and laughed. I bit the laugh off when I stumbled a little by slipping on a sand-covered rock and decided to focus on what the hell I was doing. I promised myself when this was done I would go running for a couple of hours just for the hell of it. We ran hard. About ten minutes into it I asked Keiko, "Anyone of these guys getting the feed, too?"

"No, sir."

"Why?"

There was a brief pause, not much, but enough for me to read a lot into, she told me, "Sir. They are not … qualified."

"Thanks. Out."

"*Not qualified*?" I thought. What the hell? Another mystery, but one that I didn't have time to waste brain cycles on. It was time to talk to my people, something we hadn't done to much of so far. After forty minutes of running I called a halt.

They were good. Very good. If I had them earlier the ambush of the raiding party would have been quick, and the horses would have lived to gallop another day. They sent a security team out, the rest took up positions facing outward, and everyone hydrated. All of this done with zero conversation and minimal hand signs. They moved well and blended better.

The two Captains joined me. Even though they stood in front of me, they both stood partially turned sideways so we could talk and they could scan, which they did...constantly. I started tracing the map of the school and how I wanted to approach it in the sand with the toe of my boot. As I drew a shape I named it. "Road. Fence. Buildings. School." I had no idea about how we were going to do the actual entry into the school. I was hoping that a clever ruse would occur to me. I doubted it. That would be a first, but you never know.

We took off again. I realized why going up the middle always appealed to me. It was faster. Tracing the edge of a mesa only made the trip to where I wanted start at least four times longer. It did get us there intact and unnoticed. Well, not completely unnoticed. We had a murder of crows keeping us company. That was unusual around here until Freya arrived, but even more unusual was they were still keeping their little beaks shut. I had long ago came to the conclusion that crows had a secret source of caffeine which they drank all day, and caused to them run their beaks continuously. I have a love/hate relationship with the little black feather freaks that sent a foreboding chill running down my back. The others, they loved seeing them because they knew who they belonged to. Just like the hawk that had been flying slow loops above us. They saw them as a good omen and a sign of Her Presence. For me? It grated. Why? Because Her Presence was a two-edged sword, and she had already cut me to the heart once. No way was I going to give her a second chance.

We went back to running. This time it was only for thirty minutes. Barely enough time for me to get back into the groove. We scrambled up one of the many washes coming off the mesa. In doing so, we startled a rattlesnake basking in the sun. Nobody broke stride, we just gave him some room and kept moving.

We hit the top of the mesa, and instead of us popping our heads up like a bunch of curious gophers, I stopped short and waved my squad back down a few paces. I directed the second squad to take up position at the bottom of the wash. I really hoped no one was on guard up there, or especially many others on guard. They would have the high ground and we would have to push them off it, then be exposed to the building across the road. Keiku had given me pop-up feeds, and it had looked clear. I quit buying into feeds telling me everything was looking good until I personally had seen the ground with my own eyes.

"Hit me again, Keiku."

This feed was the same as the others. I could tell by the resolution and detail that it was coming from the hawk. Crows were never that good. Their attention span was .02 seconds, and invariably something shiny distracted them. Hawks were a lot better, but every once in a while they would spot something edible on the ground below and dive. The first time that happened to me I stopped dead in my tracks, startling the squad I was leading, and braced myself for impact, all the while muttering, "Shit! Shit! Shit!" It was a mix of exhilarating and terrifying because it was so real and so sudden. Mostly terrifying.

I gestured for the 1st squad Captain to join me, popped my head up, and studied the school and the area around it while I tried to think of a plan. We were approaching the school from the back. I was looking at covered walkways painted faded blue, undoubtedly one of the school colors, that joined the two square, equally faded, boxy, white, cinder block building that were the school.

The second box was two stories high. My guess was it held the gym, cafeteria, and a handful of classrooms or storage rooms. The first box, to my right, was a one story building where the bulk of the classrooms and admin people would have their offices. The second story roof had two men with scoped wooden stock hunting rifles, probably .270's, watching. The other building's roof was empty. The front, based on the video, had the entrance to the school blocked by a school bus. The dead grass area in front of the building was quiet, and there was another school bus parked on the hard pack that passed as a lawn.

Since the birds didn't have x-ray vision, I couldn't see inside the buildings, let alone have an idea of the floor plan. I wasn't really worried about that. Once you orientated yourself inside planned structures like schools the location of everything fell into place.

I started mentally running through where I thought trouble was going to be. I was pretty sure that someone was in the bus next to the one blocking the entrance. The main entrance area would have the strongest enemy presence. More than likely set back down the main corridor and barricaded. The windows were always a possibility, especially the building with two floors. I had seen that some of the windows were broken, and the glass glittered freshly on the grass below them. It was amazing the school had managed to keep glass in the windows for so long, but then this area was barely touched by PowerDown compared to the coasts and the big desert cities like Phoenix.

I motioned for the 2nd squad Captain to join us. He acknowledged it, said something to one his people carrying a sledge strapped to his back. He slid it out of its sheath, handed it to him, and went back to watching. The Captain scrambled up to me. As he drew almost even with the rattlesnake he pivoted, took a step towards Mr. Snake, and whipped that sledge down like it was weightless. Mr. Snake took it hard. He tossed the now flat-headed rattler down to his squad and finished the rest of the space between us. He joined us, squatting on his heels next to me.

Once I would have thought spending this much time with a group like this and barely talking unusual. It was the norm now. I had met, commanded, and buried people who I spoke, at most, twenty words with in a week. The better, and longer, a team worked together the less words were needed. We hadn't spoken really, but everyone of these guys had been chattering away to each other every minute we had been together. Body language, facial expressions, how they moved, how their gear was worn, the state of their weapons and how they carried them, all that added up in my head. I had interviewed them along the way and they had done the same to

101

me. Now it was time to see how they preformed on the job. It was map in the sand time again.

Since I was going for detail, I used the tip of my bayonet to etch my sketch. The buildings remained the same. Now it was time for the master plan. I drew a sweeping half arc out to our far left. "Barrett. Roof. Then, windows with broken glass. One round below. One to the right side." I continued the arc. "Have him stop and go. Cover the buses and us." I looked at them. They both nodded. "Me and the two with the sledges go here." I indicated the side of the gym building. "We open the wall once the Barrett starts working. When you see us move in, you head to the abandoned buildings, provide suppressing fire, then, at your discretion, take the center. Clear it, then clear the other building. We'll go for the hostages. We'll join you in the center. I'm going to split them into two groups. When we come out with the kids, I'm going to keep the parent group in front. Make sure they know that I won't tolerate them breaking from the group for their kids. Explain why they have to be in front."

I stopped here and looked at them. I needed to know two things. Did they understand what I wanted, and could they stomach it? They did. They didn't like it, but that was tough shit. I wasn't too thrilled about it, either. "We'll herd the kids behind them. Push the second group of parents in tight behind and around them. I want them surrounded by adults." I paused, then continued, "They don't want to cooperate, then leave them behind." I didn't add that any non-cooperators that got in my face would be staying behind because they were dead. "The buses are the way out. Start them, one is probably good, they both look like wood-burners, load them up and go."

"Where, sir?"

"The Navajo Mountain Chapter House. I want to push them towards Rainbow Bridge. If we are going to make a stand then we might as well do it in the holy land." I grinned.

That had rhymed quite nicely. "Arm the parents when, and if, you can. Questions?" The two Captains looked at each other. Then the senior one, at least he was older, said, "Sir. It's an honor to be here with you and we want..."

"Save I,t Captain." I told him. "Get the Barrett man moving, and lets do this."

The Captain who had the Barrett guy in his sqad slid his way back down to brief his people and get them moving. I laid back and stared up at the sky, and tried to see what animal shapes I could find in the clouds floating by. I was pretty sure I had a cat cloud when the Captain quietly told me, "We're ready, sir. Give the signal?"

"You got a name, Captain?"

"Miller, sir."

"Okay. I'm Gardener. Not sir. You decide to be one of my two sledge guys?"

"Yes...Gardener."

"What's the other guy's name?"

"Rodriguez."

"Is today a good day to die, Miller?

He looked at me quizzically.

"It's not a test, Miller. Just answer."

It was a test. He knew that, too.

"It's a better day to kill."

"No shit. Lets do this thing."

# Chapter Fifteen

I don't know what the signal was supposed to be. I didn't care. I did know that over planning and fussy shit had messed up more ops than the enemy had. I came up over the edge like one of my ancestors did in the trenches of Verdun, and with a lot more success. I was still alive twenty paces later and picking up speed. I thought running along the base of the mesa was good. This was a hundred times better. This was like drinking a bottle of cold, clean well water after a couple weeks of boiled, treated, and not made any better by the addition of mint leaves liquid that poured and tasted brown. *"Oh, fuck yeah. Thank you, Freya, you bitch!"* went through my head while my eyes read every window, door, and ripple in the flow. It was rippling, no, it was twisting. The images from other hostage recovery actions in the past that I kept locked away until times like this began hammering away at the doors. My shadow-self grinned and began unlocking them for me without asking. Shadow-self knew it was time. They flowed...

*She is four. She is scared. The man with the gun tells her, "Stop the crying, kid, or I'll give you something to cry about." He grins. His grin scares her even more. She cries louder. She is terrified. He scowls, lets his rifle go, and the three point sling catches it. He moves toward her, bends down, grabs her feet, swings her in the air, and dashes her brains out against the wall.*

I am howling. The sand of the field should be slowing me down. It isn't. I am flying. My feet make contact for a blink, and I cover yards. Another...

*He doesn't want to go into the back room. Pain lives there and their smiles don't fool him. They made him shower today and he knows that is a bad, bad sign. He is prepared. His friend, the one they took last time, whispered to him about the room. He isn't going there. The piece of glass he found his pulled from his pocket. He tells himself it won't hurt that much. It doesn't, really. He has hurt worse more times than he can remember. He hopes his mom will remember him.*

In the background the Barrett booms. Good. Start up the drums and let the music begin. I can't see the center of the two buildings anymore. We are running at an angle now to the big building. The kid building. The machine gun is pumping out its staccato beat. Oh, yes. Let it begin! Other instruments begin playing. I fade them. We're against the wall. Miller is swinging his sledge. Both of them now are slamming the iron heads into the cinder block. They have done this before. Their rhythm is perfect. "Faster!" I scream. At least that is what I wanted to scream. What came out was a roar of longing, hate, and unfulfilled desire to make the men behind that wall die. They are cutting a line, one working the top, the other the bottom. In the middle, between them, the cinder block is crumbling, trembling, waiting to be shoved aside. I step back ten paces and run full tilt into it. Almost. Back. Again. I'm through. It's time to hunt.

Well, almost. I thought I was through. In an action-adventure movie from my childhood, I would have been. In those movies, no one got hung up on drywall. No, but I did. It enraged me, and I was flailing away when I was hit hard from behind and popped through the drywall. I stumbled into the room and narrowly avoided tripping over an old copier paper box filled with Christmas decorations. The light in the room went away and came back as quickly as the third man, Rodriquez, passed through the hole. I looked at them, listened to what I could hear on the other side of the door, which was boots running, grabbed the door handle, and hit the hallway, hugging the right side as I did. I had Sword out, my audio read of the boot heels had them twenty feet down from the door as I exited. My peripheral vision registered Miller taking the opposite side of the hallway giving us both clear lanes while Rodriguez, I knew without looking, was facing the other way behind us, covering our backs.

It was funny, the expression on the three Apaches faces, charging down the hall, now maybe eight paces from us, when they saw us pop out of the door. So funny that I laughed. Then I stepped forward and swung Sword overhand and down at an angle, catching the lead Apache on the collarbone and slicing down and in. Sword was a Sword 1.0 version, which meant it had no groove in the blade. It had a tendency to get stuck when skewering people. Usually only when you needed it not to. So, I sliced instead. It was also more fun. As the blade connected I yelled, "Freya!" Let go of Sword, stepped into the lane of the man on my right, and kicked that Apache in the balls. Then I drew my right-hand Ruger and shot him. The kicking in the balls part could have been skipped, but I got as much fun from doing it as I had slicing his partner.

In the background I heard the 2nd squad machine gun open up and the burst of a hand grenade. I'd never heard one of the new ones they were carrying go off, so I couldn't positively identify the sound, but I hoped they were the only ones with them. I also hoped they didn't kill off all the hostages saving them. I knew we were going to take casualties

106

among them, I just didn't want any screamers until we got everyone loaded up and moving. It wasn't what I wanted, and I didn't look forward to it as I had a real problem dealing mentally with wounded and dead kids. I would, and had. It was lock it away and keep rolling. That worked until you were alone or drifted off to sleep. Then it all came back, and uglier if possible.                    All this was running through my head while I worked on orientating myself. I was about to lead us back the way Rodriquez was facing when I heard a kid scream from the opposite direction. The same one the three Apaches had come from. I started running in that direction. The scream which, in my head at least, had never stopped.

The only thing I did right next was take the corner wide. I wasn't thinking anymore. I was slipping away fast to a place I had only come close to, and not all that often in the past few years, the place where I didn't give a shit. I didn't think. I didn't care. Where everything happened in slow motion around me, where only one thing mattered, and that was to kill. I had already tasted it today, now I gulped it and I loved it. I only slowed down when I made the left at the corridor leading to the open double doors of the gym, because I was trying to avoid falling on my ass.

I did register amazement that somehow, someone, had managed to keep a shine on the floor. The shine, and the blood puddles I had run through to get this far, combined to save my life. I slid, went down on a knee and skidded into the lockers that lined the wall as one of the two guys standing further down the hallway sent three rounds into the space I had just occupied. I, in turn, sent one round that was hand loaded especially for me, a .357 hollow point, into his throat. He dropped and flopped ugly.

Miller and Rodriguez did it differently. They used the

107

corner I had just raced around for partial cover and a high/low look around. One of them, maybe Rodriguez, took out the second man. His was a head shot. The floor was going to be slippery here for a while. Whoever did the floor waxing here was going to be very unhappy. I yelled, "Freya!" and heard it echoed by Miller and Rodriguez. Then I hauled ass through the open doors. For good measure I yelled, "Freya!" again. I was feeling all warm and fuzzy for the blond bitch for giving me my body back.

What I saw surprised me and iced me right back down. The gym was big and made bigger by the little kids, who were standing with their bigger sisters and brothers in pockets. Not that any of the older ones were all that big, anyway. There wasn't very many of them. I expected, I don't know why, that there would be at least thirty plus kids. Instead there was twelve. Really eleven, number twelve was a little girl held by a Apache who had a gun to her head. Ten paces away on his right stood another Apache with an AK who seemed really unsure about where to point the barrel. At the kids, me, or Miller and Rodriguez who had come in behind me. I slowed down to a walk, and time slowed to a crawl.

"Hey asshole. Put the gun down."

"Who the fuck are you, white man?"

I looked at him, at the gun he was holding nice and steady, and the little girl who was giving me the, "Save me!" eyes. I winked and smiled at her while, "*My life is going full circle,*" passed through my head.

"Gardener."

Then I shot him right between the eyes. The kid would need someone to talk to later, but she was alive to do it. Somebody would have to clean her off first before she did, and it wouldn't be me. The wavering Apache with the AK decided to shoot, too. His target was me, and he hit it. It hurt, too. No delay of pain on this one. I knew right away I had been hit, and hit bad. He had been at an angle to me, and the round punched thru my left shoulder, high up. Any higher and a little more over, and I would have taken it in the neck, shattering bone before exiting out the back. Of course, it was where the gap in my body armor coverage was. The rest of his rounds went high, and he was probably dead before he hit the floor. Miller and Rodriguez both made sure of that. The Ruger I held in my left hand dropped to the ground. I couldn't hold it any longer. I couldn't hold my arm up, either. "Fuck! So much for the functioning body!" I barked, "Get these kids moving." Miller and Rodriguez were staring at me, the horrified looks on their faces was almost amusing. I added, "Now!" Rodriguez told the kids, "Okay. Lets go find some parents, but we need to be fast, quiet, and do what you're told. Got it?"

Miller didn't listen to me. I didn't really expect him to. Instead, he hustled over to me, took a quick look, and started cutting away my shirt. "Give me your bandage." He fished out his, and yelled the same thing at Rodriquez. I awkwardly fished mine out and handed it to him. Rodriguez got close enough to check out the damage, shot a look at Miller, tossed him his wound dressing, and started moving kids.

He yelled, "Single file, inside voices, oldest at the rear. Lets go, people!"

"We got to go, Miller."

"Shut up, Gardener."

That set me back. I felt anger flare, then I laughed and asked him, "That bad?" He ignored that. Instead, he told me, "Hang on. Almost done." He cut away part of his left leg trouser and used the fabric to bind the wound bandages in place. "Okay, Gardener. I got morphine. You want some?"

"No."

"You think you're going to go into shock, let me know."

"Yeah. Lets go."

He took the lead after grabbing the AK, slinging it, and

pulling a magazine from the asshole that shot me. Sweet Jesus, the pain was talking to me. I ran my mental pain killer routines, I had a high tolerance for it, having experienced more then my share, but this was bad. We made it about ten paces when I yelled to Miller, "Take drag. I'm going up front with Rodriquez." He started to say something, changed his mind, and scowled at me as I went past. As I passed the kids I checked them out. Some of them looked scared, but most of them looked bored. One of the boys, maybe 12, quietly called out to me, "Give me a gun, mister. I can shoot."

"Later, kid."

I saw Rodriguez drop to a knee, look around the corner, then let rip with a full auto burst. He ducked back, grinned at me, pulled a grenade, twisted the bottom, and tossed it skittering along the floor. It made for a nice satisfying scream a couple of beats later. He jumped out, let go with one three round burst, and moved out. I caught up and took the other side of the hall. If going into the gym was messy, this was a lot worse. No body parts blown off, but the four Apaches in the hallway were leaking blood from a lot of different places. Mixed in with the blood on the floor were nickel-sized pieces of metal. I heard the kids murmuring and thought my hearing had been scrambled until I realized it was *Dine* they were speaking.

Now came the tricky part, the linkup with our people. This was where, if done wrong, or even right, sometimes a dumb ass would shoot you because they were jumpy. We pulled it off with minimal shouting and zero shooting. Kat came running up to me. I was pleased to see the relief on her face that I was still alive, but I didn't like the concern when she saw I was hit.

"Oh my god! You've been shot!"

If she asked me, "Does it hurt?" it was going to be really hard to resist the urge to knock her upside the head. I hurt, hurt badly, and it was making me short-tempered. Instead she asked me, "Did you kill the asshole?"

"No. Rodriguez did."

I wasn't sure of that. Was it him, or Miller? I was having problems concentrating. "Do the buses have first-aid kits?"

"I don't know. I can check."

"Good. Do it."

I wasn't the only one hurt. 2nd squad had one with a leg wound, and one of the parents was dying. Not bad work. Miller was getting everyone moving. The parents, instead of being mindless cattle bitching about whatever was on their little minds, were helping. I could remember a time when that would have been a miracle. Now it was a rarity.

"You got a bus started yet, Miller?"

"No, sir."

"Get somebody on it. I want to move."

"Got it."

"Then get back to me. I want a sitrep."

I couldn't help notice how everyone was checking me out without trying to be obvious about it. "*Fuck 'em,*" I thought. I watched 2nd squad take up watch positions, and figured it was time to check in with the eye in the sky.


"Hey, Keiku. Show me the town." I got nothing.

"Keiku?"

Damn. I needed this like I needed a shattered arm joint, or whatever the hell it was.

"Keiku."

I used my command voice. I always laughed inside when I did. People either listened to you or they didn't. If they didn't -- well, it was their loss. Sometimes of their life.

"Sorry, sir. I'm here."

She hesitated, more than likely she never noticed it, but

111

I did.

"I've been tasked elsewhere."

"Fine." It wasn't, but life rarely went smoothly.

"Give me the city from up high and work north a bit."

"Roger that. Stand by. And, sir..."

"What?"

"This will be the final feed."

"Then make it so, Keiku."

She hit me with the image feed. Mr Hawk was riding a thermal, so it took me a second to orientate myself, and when I did, I didn't like what I saw. The bulk of the Apaches had given up on their siege of the bridge and were heading this way. Yeah, it was time to go. I grayed out for a second. When I refocused, Miller was standing in front of me saying, "Time to go, Gardener." He reached out to steady me and I snapped at him, "Sitrep, Captain. Have our wounded been taken care of?"

"Johnson, the Barrett guy, he's our team medic. He just got in, and he'll see you first."

"Bullshit. He'll take care of the others first. Are we ready to roll?"

"Yes, sir. We're waiting on you."

I looked around. Where had all the people gone? Damn, I needed to get it together. In a softer voice Miller said, "What did you see?"

"Incoming traffic. We need to haul ass."

"How much of a lead do we have?"

"We have a Plan B type of lead, Captain."

Miller looked at me, shook his head, and walked away flashing hand signs to pull the security team in. I couldn't move. I was leaning against the side of the school building watching without watching. I couldn't focus, all I was able to do was observe. What was hovering around inside me was the desire to just drift off like a balloon. I knew I had felt this before, sometime, somewhere, I just couldn't remember where.

Miller had stopped. He was staring at me, then gesturing for me to move. It was time to go. I wasn't sure I wanted to. It wasn't fear or lassitude, it was the realization that if I moved, my world would move on, too. I wasn't sure how, I just knew it. I looked past Miller at the bus. Smoke was belching from the crude stack at the back as the wood fired engine came up to speed. Kat stood in the door, concern on her face. I knew any second she would be off the bus and running to me. From the windows I saw the faces, the faces of children, and so I moved. In doing so, something snapped inside of me. Clarity returned. The pain stayed, but I could live with that for now.

I jogged to the bus, which began moving when I was within five paces of it. Kat was there to meet me, as was Miller. I ignored her look of concern. "Kat, I want an adult next to the windows and the kids next to them. Miller, space our people out between them. I want you and Rodriguez up front here with me, ready to go." The wood-burning machinery took up all the space in the back, so we had that working for us. I wanted to keep the ring of bodies around them for as long as possible. The Barrett guy pushed pass Miller, and Kat and told me, "Take a seat. Let's check out the damage." They had kept a seat open for me behind the driver. I sat down, and he started peeling off the wound bandages. I looked down and saw the white of splintered bone. I looked away, but not before seeing his eyes change. I knew. He knew. I would be lucky to have a stump left.

# Chapter Sixteen

"Talk to me, Miller."

"Sir, we lost four adult locals inside. Two have minor wounds. Sargent Kim has a leg wound. He is good for the next 48 hours. We are good for one engagement as far as ammo goes. Your turn."

"We are being pursued, or will be shortly, by the remains of the unit that was trying to take the bridge."

I didn't want to tell them I had been dropped by the big picture people. I had learned about morale and how important it was to act like we had the winning hand even when I knew we didn't. I did the math, compared my estimate of their speed to ours, and came to a conclusion I wasn't ready to share yet.

"We're good."

I had to stop talking and grit my teeth. Whatever he did had just hurt like a bitch. Just as that passed, we hit a road crater, my arm moved, and the pain returned just as bad. When I felt I could talk again, I said, "Hey, medic. You got a name?"

"Cat Daddy."

"Bind the arm to me."

He looked at me. With the exception of Kat, the rest had looked away. I stared at him until he said, "Fine. Hang on. I got to dump some magic potion on it and then wrap it." I braced myself for the pain of the magic potion. It was the right thing to do. This time it was bad enough that I almost threw up on my recently repaired boots. Life was good sometimes. I grayed out again. When I came back the medic was gone, and Miller was sitting next to me. He said quietly, "You don't have to do this."

"What?"

He didn't say anything for a minute. Then, just as quietly he said, "Legion Commander Ninja..." I cut him off. I would have laughed, but I didn't feel like it, "Don't call him that. I am not in the mood for it. His name is Ninja." He got over being taken aback and continued, "He asked for volunteers, only males who had sons were eligible, we volunteered to a man. After he chose us, we had a good idea it would be us, he sent us to see...Max. He looked at us, said one word, then dismissed us." I couldn't think of what Max would have told them, especially in one word, so I told him what I came up with, "He said apple pie?" He looked at me strangely and then laughed. "No." He paused, then said, "That's two words. No,he said 'Thermopylae'." I thought about it. My mind flashing back to a really lame movie I had once watched in a land and time that was now long gone. There were worse ways to end it.

Funny thing was, I had run a few images through my and realized the road narrowed between a couple of sandstone formations a few miles before the chapter house. Someone was going to have to slow the assholes down behind us, and I couldn't think of a better place to do it. I told him about it an asked him, "You up to it?" He shrugged, "If it isn't going to be here, it'll be somewhere else."

"The same as before, plus one of your choice. Give them an out. Load up. Especially water." He grinned. "Hell, who knows. Maybe it'll have a happy ending."

"Go away, Miller. Find the medic and bring me some me pain killers."

I leaned my head back and let my mind idle. That didn't work out so well. Fat, nasty thoughts with swollen bellies crept out from under the rocks and began whispering, "*You're a cripple. You're a cripple*," or, "*You're going to die!*" I didn't mind the dying taunts. The cripple ones I could have done with out. I gave up. I looked out the window and was watching the passing nothing when Kat slid into the empty space next to me.                     She didn't say anything. She just held out her hand, opened it, and I recognized the two yellow footballs on it.

I took them, dry swallowed them, started choking, and drank from the water bottle she handed me. "Thanks." I closed my eyes again. I was hoping she would go away. She didn't. I waited for a couple of minutes. I was going to have to get ready to go in about twenty minutes. I wanted to ride the Oxy until then. Not talk. Without opening my eyes I told her, "Usually when someone closes their eyes it means they want you to go away."

"That's not always true. You could just be sleepy."

"I'm not."

She thought about that, but she didn't move. Instead she said, "I know what you're going to do." I opened my eyes and stared straight ahead. "I don't know what I'm going to do. It's kinda like how I lead my life. So, you don't know." She didn't argue. Instead she said, "Look at me." I looked at her, and she kissed me hard on the lips and whispered, "Goodbye. You were the best."

"*Were?*" Echoed in my head. I banished it. I didn't have time to dwell on shit like that right now. I went back to watching nothing roll past and what kind of load out we'd need. It was time in no time. It wasn't always that way. I used to count the seconds before an action. This time they just rolled by me, almost unnoticed. I must have drifted away, because all of sudden Miller was sitting next to me and repeating my name.

"What, Miller?"

"Time to do it."

"Fuck. Okay. I want our people to each have two hundred fifty rounds, all the water they can carry, and nothing else. I want the Barrett guy..." I tried to remember his name, shit it was gone, "...to come with us, too. Also..."

He cut me off, firmly, quietly, but never the less, he cut me off. "I did all that. We're out of .50 caliber, and we don't have two hundred fifty rounds per man, unless you want to send 2nd Squad away with three magazines apiece."

"You burned though that much ammo?"

"No. We came light. Had to. We were going for speed and humping heavy hardware. We look good for the SAW, but otherwise we go with what we got." The bus was slowing. "Okay, Miller. Block the road with the bus. Get everyone moving towards the chapter house on foot. Two miles is less then twenty minutes. The terrain is too rough for anyone to follow by vehicle after they get past there. Let 2nd Squad do the rearguard action."

"I've already arranged for all that, Gardener." I thought about that. "So, whats left, Captain?"

"Our jobs, sir."

I had to laugh at that. "Yeah. You got that right."

I was the first off the bus. That was part of the job, too. I stood off to one side with Miller. As Rodriguez, and the guy with the SAW, got off they would pause, look around, stare at a spot, and look at Miller. He would nod and they would take off.

The people themselves? The men looked grim, the women stone faced, and the kids excited. Each adult took a second to try and smile at me or nod. No words. Just that. 2nd squad kept them moving. As they passed me, they each saluted. That was more than a little strange. I didn't return it. I nodded. I knew how to salute, I just never felt right doing it. Their Captain joined me and Miller, and we all watched Kat

118

get off the bus. She didn't say anything to me. She just kept on going. I guess she figured she said all she had to say. She might have, but I hadn't. I called her name and watched as she reluctantly turned around. She was crying. I gestured for her to come to me. She didn't bother to wipe away the tears when she stood in front of me. She just looked at me. "Here." I pulled the Colt Navy out of my belt and handed to her.

"Why me?"

"Why not?"

She almost smiled, almost said something, but instead she turned and ran off. She did have a great ass. "Time for me go, sir." It was the other Captain. "Okay." I mean, what was the deal here with everyone? Just go. Hell, we didn't have time for this. I was getting that feeling, the one that told me it was time to get ready for the storm. He saluted me, and then said, "It's an honor. I envy you, Miller."

"Right." I told him. "Get your ass out of here." He grinned and was gone too.

"Okay, Miller. You need to salute or anything?'

"No, Gardener."

"Good. Pick a spot and go find it."

He looked at me like he was going to say something profound or worse. "Just do it." I walked off. I knew where I was going and what I was going to do. Maybe drugs weren't that bad after all.

# Chapter Seventeen

Everyone was gone with the exception of Miller, who had decided, without asking, to stay on the road with me. The squad, such as it was, was either scrambling up the sandstone the road was cut through, or already out of sight. I looked around. It was a beautiful day, and far away from any place I called home. As soon as I thought that, I had to laugh. I had no home. I just had places memories had happened in. If this all worked out, then this would be another one.

The road had been cut through a sandstone outcropping, each side was ragged but climbable straight up for about fifteen feet. That was why I was down on the road with the bus. No way in hell I was going to climb that today. I walked over to the rear wheel and sat down with my back against it. The way the bus was parked made where I was sitting the only gap between it and the sandstone. If I stayed beyond the wheel I wouldn't be seen, and I would have some protection against incoming rounds. It was a plan. Not much of one, I had to admit, but a plan. I was never all that good with a rifle, anyway. If I was going to make a difference, it would have to wait until they got in close. Miller took the other wheel, and began laying out his magazines and grenades.

"You want a grenade or two, Gardener?"

"No."

I waited a minute or two and asked him, "What the hell you doing here Miller?"

"Down here with you?  My job."

"No.  I mean riding to the rescue."

"Well, there was what they told us and what I think is going on."

"Explain, Miller."

"You're a big deal, hell, you're a legend.  Everyone knows you, or thinks they do."

"But there is another reason.  Right, Miller?"

"Yeah, it's how things are run and done these days."

He didn't sound too happy about it, either.  "It was a lot simpler when I started doing this.  What I think is that in the big picture we're here to win the hearts and minds of the Navajo.  This area, and the people in it, are in the right place for the move to take back the rest of the west coast, you know, the place that used to be Southern California."

"Yeah.  Max always thought big.  He wants it all. Him and Freya."

He shrugged.  "What we leave behind is always better then what we found." I laughed.  "Sure it is.  After you've killed most of the people who might disagree with you, it is easy to set things in order."

"Isn't that what you do?"

He had a point.  I didn't answer him.  I didn't feel like I needed to.  It didn't matter, anyway.

We had some time.  At least ten minutes, which was good.  I was tired.  I was also cold, probably because I was in the shade.  I thought about moving into the sun, but it wasn't worth it.  I wondered how Ninja was doing.  It would be good to see him and Max again.  Maybe after this I would go North and see them.  Hell, the way they were moving I could go back to Virginia.  I liked that even better.  I missed Virginia, or whatever it was called now.  I didn't like to think about it, but I had outlived, lost, or moved away from everything that meant something to me.  I was glad when I heard the sound of engines. It killed what was turning into a really morbid line of thought. My guess was they had scouts running ahead of the main body on motorcycles. I closed my eyes again. Miller's people could handle this. They did. I didn't even bother to look. I just listened and saw it unfold.

Two outriders, both going faster than they should have been, saw the bus and slowed down later than they should have. They got the part where only one approaches while the other hangs back almost right. Almost in that the one who hung back thought he was out of range from whoever was at the bus ambush. He wasn't. His partner went down about thirty paces from me. Miller rolled out from behind the wheel and shot him from under the bus. The SAW reached out and finished his partner before he could get headed back to warn the main body.

Miller gave me a thumbs up, crawled under the bus, and went out to salvage, drag bodies, and push the bikes off the road. The main body had better be moving fast, because there wasn't time to dig holes and there wasn't much to cover them. They would spot them, no doubt about that, the question was if they had a point vehicle who would warn them, or they would all just run down the road, spot the leftovers on the side, and pull up and gawk. If they did, the SAW would light up the lead and end vehicle. Maybe we could get a traffic jam and do some serious damage before they got their shit together and ran us over like the speed bump we were.

I didn't have any illusions about what was going to happen here. I just wanted to have fun while I could. The fun arrived maybe fifteen minutes later. I heard them coming, once again I had slipped away, and did a gut check to see what I had left. It had been nice to feel young, far too fleeting, like my youth had been. I smiled. I liked it when I thought profound shit like that. I figured I had enough left in the tank. If I didn't, I would pretend until I did.

It was easy to hear them coming because they must have pulled everything they had that had wheels and was still running from the bridge siege. I almost felt flattered. Then I realized that if they kept going they would end up in the spiritual heart of the Navajo and Hopi people. Damn, strategic thinking made my head hurt. So did all their fucking noise. Miller had been checking our new arrivals out, peering around the tire. When he pulled his head back and looked at me, I knew it was grim. His face told me that. So I had to take a look. He was right. I felt even better. I liked grim.

What I had seen was pretty grim. Our SAW opened up on them, but the lead vehicle, tail vehicle plan was toast. They were good. Instead of bunching up, they had fanned out in an arc, with their vehicles not off-road capable either tucked in behind the lead element or reversing as quickly as possible back down the road. Those were the vehicles the SAW had targeted. I mentally agreed with their choice. Why? Those had to be their supply carriers. It wouldn't help us here, but it would help those that came after us.

Living off the land wasn't a viable option for an occupier here. Mechanized warfare with a high ammo burn rate was a rarity nowadays for a reason. I doubted if the Saints could maintain more than three mobile units like this for long in the field, and they had the resources of a state. The Apaches must be far more desperate than most knew. They had two, maybe three, mounted .50 calibers, two most definitely, each mounted on ancient Humvee's. Both answered our SAW and provided cover for the dismounts racing across the dead land to the SAW position. Yes, there was a third one, a .30 caliber, which was more than sufficient. It ripped a line across the bus body and provided coverage for our very own team of dismounts heading for us.

That's when the two Bic's arrowed in, passing over our heads, screaming like predatory birds from a caveman's nightmare. Bic's were the poor state's answer to the Fed's drones. They were called "Bic's" because you used them and threw them away. I thought they should have been called matches because you usually only got one light from them before they blew out, but no one had asked me. They were cheaply made, lacked most of the high-end capabilities, couldn't fly as high, or carry the same armaments as the Fed's drones did. The screaming came from modified deer collusion avoidance devices, that someone who had played one too many World War II computer games had designed for them.

Immediately every hostile weapon was pointed at them in hopes of hosing them from the air. Sometimes it worked. I had seen it done once and privately though it was pure luck, while publicly congratulating the woman who did it. Miller was delighted to see them. He was screaming, "Yeah! Freya!" Freya had nothing to do with it.

I recognized the stylized beehive of the Saints painted on the fuselage. I also knew it was nice that they cared enough to send them, but I also knew it wasn't going to be enough. They were too late, the dismounts were already out of their kill zone. I took a quick look at what was headed our way. The dismounts were either trying to bring their weapon up and hit one of the Bic's, or hauling ass towards me and Miller. *"Damn, some of these guys looked young to be out here,"* went through my head. Then the Bic's did their thing, and it was beautiful to see when it wasn't happening to you.

Bic's carried two antitank tubes that fired the equivalent of a shoulder-launched antitank weapon, which is what the design was copied from. State-of-the-art almost fifty years ago, it was state-of-the-art once again. Only three worked, not unusual. The fourth one failed to launch, and instead dropped like a stone. Often the remote operator, if ordered to do so, would use the Bic itself as a rocket, and dive it into a target. I heard it happen instead of watching it. I had left my head in sight for a couple beats too long and almost had a chunk blown out by someone who was paying attention to the job and not the air show. I pulled it back and got ready for the first arrivals. They weren't long in arriving.

The first wave arrived pretty much together. There were five of them. Three took my side, it must have looked easier, two tried going over the hood of the bus on Miller's side. My left arm kept trying to move on its own. I wished it didn't, because it hurt when it did. I waited until I heard them about five paces from hitting the gap, and started backpedaling away from the wheel and at an angle away from where they would be coming out. I didn't worry about Miller. He was good enough to do what was needed and if he didn't, well, life was like that sometimes. The first one came through fast and hard. His eyes were white and big, and he was breathing hard, probably more from adrenalin than the run.

I shot him in the head and charged him. His motor kept running for a couple of beats, all I needed. I kicked him in the chest, driving him back into the two behind him and shot them, not as cleanly as I did the first, but good enough for me to still keep breathing until the next batch hit the hole. I was hoping they would all pile up in the gap and create a body wall, but it didn't happen. Instead they sprawled. One, the first inside and where he needed to be, the other two just outside of it. Miller had handled his two. One he left draped over the hood, the other he was busy stuffing underneath the bus to catch bullets.

He twisted the releases on two of those German style hand grenades and lobbed them over the bus. I dropped behind the wheel again and waited for the "bang!"s. He timed it right from the cries of pain, but they also blew out what remained of the windows. I wasn't hearing the SAW anymore. I didn't think I would ever again. That's when someone on the other side got smart. They rolled a grenade under the bus. It came to a stop between me and Miller. He didn't hesitate. I did, and he dived for it, covering it with his body. The results weren't pretty. I quit hesitating. It was time. I ran at the gap, leaping bodies, and came out the other side looking for targets. My armor took two hits right away. I shot one of the shooters in the chest, cocked and shot some guy just as he let go with a three round burst that walked up my right side, starting at mid thigh. I staggered backwards, there were too many targets and I only had one gun, one hand, and one thought, which I screamed, *"Fuck you!"* I was hit again, hard, and I focused on the nearest target. He was maybe fourteen at best, and from the look on his face he hated my guts. He had a revolver pointed at me, the fucking bore looked huge. I didn't pull the trigger. He did. My mouth exploded, and I tasted my blood before it went black.

# Epilogue

I was lying on something soft. It smelled good, too. Not as good as the smell of the woman whose hair was brushing my face. I knew that smell. I didn't open my eyes. I just whispered her name, "Night..."

"You were expecting someone else?" I opened my eyes. It was her. She was smiling at me. Her face unmarked, her eyes bright. No blood, no bone fragments.

"Night!"

"Hush."

A little later I asked her, "Is this heaven?"

"Yes."

I rolled on top of her and whispered, "Do they know I'm here?"

"I think so." She put her finger to my lips. "We'll have plenty of time to talk later."

Made in the USA
San Bernardino, CA
01 December 2012